Maliek Part Two

Copyright © 2015 by Katreka Carter

All rights reserved. This book or any portion thereof may not be reproduced or used in any manner whatsoever without the express written permission of the publisher except for the use of brief quotations in a book review.

ISBN: 978-1530482863

Chapter 1

As the young girl sat next to her mother's bed with tears streaming down her face. "Don't leave me mommy. What will I do? Grandma is not able to take care of me." Her mother squeezed her hand and said "be strong. I'm sorry baby". Her eyes just looked into the ceiling and slowly faded away. The little girl laid her hand on her chest and sobbed uncontrollably. Her grandma took her hand. "Baby she is gone and everything will be ok. I promise you. God will make a way for us to survive. Your mama is in a better place now. "

"Well, grandma what are we going to do? I'll be old enough to get a job in a few months." Soon after her mom's death, she started applying for jobs while attending school. She landed a job as a waitress in a soul food restaurant. Now at least they could make ends meet. Two years later, her grandma passed, and she was left alone to take care of herself. She had a good neighbor that was just like a mother to her. She soon began calling her "Nana". One afternoon she was sitting with Nana drinking tea. "Now that my grandma is gone, are you sure it's ok to call you Nana?"

"Sure." She replied. I know that your granny would have wanted it this way. We have been friends for a very long time now. I met your grandma at a club one night. She caught her old man cheating. He told her he was going to be out to town for a few days and she wasn't the every week bar hopper so she decided to go out. When she arrived at the club I was sitting at the bar. She must have saw them sitting in the corner. She asked the bartender for a bottle of wine then turned to me as asked me to watch her purse. When I looked around, she had poured wine all over the two of them and snatched the lady's wig off. All you heard was Jake saying "Esther, Esther what are you doing? Let me explain." Well, the lady didn't hang around to hear anymore. She was too embarrassed at the way he looked at her after her wig went flying across the room! After it was all over, we drank and laughed all night. We became the best of friends from that day on. But your grandma used to always say "Honey I'm going to church and find me a man." And, girl she did. That was your grand dad, Victor Mann. The perfect couple. They went to church so much I started going trying to find me a Victor Mann. He was so good to her. He bought her the house she left you right next to me. I sure do miss her." Desarie hugged Nana. "I'm so glad that you were here. I don't know what I would do without you." Desarie didn't feel so alone anymore. One day she was going through her Mother's and Grandma's belongings so she could donate them. She found some letters with a rubber band wrapped around them. All of the letters had return to sender stamped on the front. She opened the first one; it read "Dear James, I heard that you have gotten married and started preaching. And, that's good, but I don't know how to tell you but the last night we spent together before you left to go to the army, we conceived a child, and she's a beautiful girl. She looks a lot like you. Her name is Desarie. She is now five years old. I am sorry, I didn't tell you sooner but I didn't want to cause any problems with you and your wife and two sons. We have made it this far. Good luck, love". She read another letter saying that she wanted him to meet his daughter and that she was sick and didn't know how long she was going to live. "I know you are opening all of my letters and returning them. How could you do this to her and you are supposed to be a man of God? Now at this moment Desarie finally knew who her father was after all these years, James Turner II. As she continued to read the letters Desarie cried at the thought of her never having the chance to meet her father. Her mother never wanted to discuss this with her. Every time she brought the subject up, she would brush her off and tell her that it is not important. She is her mom and dad. She ran out of time, plus, at this point she was too upset to read anymore. She put the letters in the top drawer and got ready for work. "I'll finish this when I get back", she said closing the drawer.

Chapter 2

Desarie's job wasn't very far from where she lived, so she usually enjoyed walking to work during the summer months. In the winter, she would take a cab or bus. Locking the door behind her she, she left walking, when she reached the third block a Malibu Classic drove up and she stopped in her tracks looking at a handsome young man sitting behind the wheel. "Can I give you a ride", he said showing a Colgate smile. "Now do I look like the type of girl that will just jump in anyone's car and with anybody? Remember this is Detroit not Flint. You must not be from here", she said walking slow. "Yes, I am but, I'm from the east side, born and raised", he said jumping on and off his gas petal. She kept walking down Boston St until, she reached Woodward. He was still following her. She turned around and looked at him again. "What are you some type of psycho or something?" "No", he exclaimed. I am just trying to get to know you."

"Well I am not trying to meet no one". He didn't reply but watched her knowing that she was more than an attraction to him. Des always wore short skirts showing off her nice shapely legs she inherited from her mom and grandma. Her clothes didn't have to be name brand because she looked good in anything she wore. She had that kind of shape. She was a very neat dresser. Her grandma taught her how you could go in the thrift shop and pick up nice things, put them in the dry cleaners to make them look new, and no one would know that you bought it from there. He followed her all the way to work, parking his car watching her go into Dave's which is a very popular soul food restaurant in the metro area. All day, there were gamblers, drug hustlers, number writers and who ever made money, came there to eat the food which was habit forming. And what most people needed after a hard night hustling is a good meal even if a person had took a lost, Dave would feed them anyway. They could pay him later. He knew a good hustler would not stay down long. Once Desarie started working full time, she made plenty of money. Her tips were so much sometimes until she was able to help Nana with her small bills. CJ walked into the restaurant and was seated by Dave's wife. "Sir would you like smoking or none?" He looked around the restaurant and saw which section she was working and noticed a man smoking. Removing his hat, "smoking" he said following behind her with a smirk on his face. Desarie walked to the table, "what can I get you today?"

"You can get me an address and phone number for starts."

"Ok I guess you have noticed we sell food here not phone numbers, and don't you think if I was interested in you I would have jumped in the car with you?" He got so insulted by the statement until he picked up his Detroit Pistons cap and walked out of the restaurant. Reality set in after seeing him leave. "Maybe I shouldn't have been so rude to him the brother was truly fine. I am not looking for no man even though I need one. When I do get one, he better have some money or making some on a daily basis." The day went by fast and Des was tired leaving work. She headed home once she got to the corner of her street, CJ was sitting in a Cadillac Sedan De Ville waiting. He hollered out of his window "Hey you stop acting so stuck up and at least give me a chance to holler at you. I've been watching you for a while now and I know for sure, you don't have a man." That really hit a spot. "Just because you don't see me with one, doesn't mean that I don't have one." "Well just let me give you a ride. I'm sure your man would appreciate that", he said sarcastically. He couldn't help but laugh after he said that plus her feet was tired and what harm could a ride do? Plus, she already noticed the fact he was driving a different car and a caddy at that. She knew then, he wasn't a broke man. She accepted the ride and from that day, they started seeing each other. Desarie soon fell head over heels in love with CJ. He was a good hustler and tried to keep a job working in several clubs and the reason for this is he could do his business on the side. He would always say "my best customers hang out in bars."

Chapter 3

One night after a long day at work, CJ dropped her off at home. She began reading the letters again, "yeah I saw you and your family. I see you have two boys and they seem to be real close age wise to Des. Don't you think it's about time that you acknowledge your offspring? Why are you returning my letters or is it your wife? Remember God don't like ugly." All of this stuck in her mind. She questioned why was I deprived and he has other kids. She started to become real bitter. A few years later, Des ended up marrying CJ. He was a good provider. He moved her into another house, but she never sold her house that was left by her granny which was a smart idea. You never know what a man might do and she will always have something to fall back on. She trusted her husband so much until she confided in him about the letters. He saw the way it upset her and made her sad from even the conversation. He didn't take it too well. He looked at it as a vendetta. He ran around investigating and found out all the information he could about the Turner family. He told her that her father had passed and that her brothers live very large. Also found out that one of her brothers was opening up a large club (club stallion). She told him, she wanted to find out everything about both of them! CJ had different thoughts in his mind. "So CJ you are telling me one of my brothers is a baller and the other one is a preacher?"

"Yes, Des but the Rev hasn't always been a Reverend". After hearing all of their successes and accomplishments, she began to feel a sense of jealousy, thinking maybe her father would have had a different impact on her life if he had given her a chance to meet him and her two brothers. Kissing her gently on her lips, "baby you don't have to worry about anything. I will get a job at his club and let you know everything about him". True enough, CJ got a job at Club Stallion. Maliek paid him very well and liked the way he worked with the customers. Before long CJ started to drink real heavy constantly every night after he got off from work. By now, Des had Juquan and was tired of him and his drunken ways. He would say all sorts of things under the influence. He would turn into another person and not the one she fell in love with and married. He would wake up the next day as if nothing happened and this wasn't a good thing for their son to see constantly, time after time. One night CJ clowned so bad, the next day, she waited until he left for work and packed all of her and her son things and moved back into her house. On her way, she said "oh boy, I am so glad I didn't let him talk me into selling my house." When CJ found them gone, he came over to her house and Nana met him with a shotgun, as he was getting out of his car. "Don't try it. Don't you think you have put them through enough?"

"Move old lady, I am not scared of no gun", thinking she was bluffing. Des heard the commotion and ran to the door. "CJ what are you doing here? Don't come to my house around me and my son until you clean up your act". Nana cocked the gun and he started backing up.

"Des, this is not over. I have gave you everything. I want to raise my son".
"CJ just leave". He finally got in his car. Eyeing the shotgun and drove off fast burning rubber. "Chile go on back in the house. I will not let him ever hurt you or that boy."

Chapter 4
(Charlie Jackson aka CJ)

CJ sat in his room counting his money over and over. Thinking about only if he could have caught Doug he would have had an extra million dollars. "Now I have to go shopping so that I can change my whole appearance". He turned on the television and saw a special broadcast airing his name and a picture of Doug. "I knew that dummy would get caught I should have killed him when I had the chance." His heart began to flutter thinking about all the information that Doug could give them on him and the kidnapping. I know he is going to sing like a mocking bird after seeing this. He grabbed the duffel bag and suitcase leaving the hotel out of the back entrance. When he walked to the main street, he hailed a taxi. "I will pay you extra if you drive me to a couple of stores and wait while I do a little shopping". He pulled out one hundred dollars and gave it to the driver. "I will wait for you", the driver said with a smile. He knew this was a good trip. Probably enough for him to take the rest of the day off. Once CJ had purchased everything he needed, he got back in the taxi. "Could you take me to a hotel where I can rent the room by the hour? I should be leaving Canada soon and there is no sense in renting a room for the whole night." The driver didn't say anything but nodded his head and drove him to the Canadian Inn which was a small secluded motel sitting in a vicinity alone. He paid the driver another fifty dollars, grabbed his bags and got out of the cab. The driver passed him a card. "If you need ride call me." It was clear he didn't speak English too well. CJ walked inside the hotel. He walked to the window. The clerk was sitting with his legs propped up on the desk reading. CJ cleared his throat. That didn't move him so he rang the bell. The clerk got up and walked to the window. "I need a room for a couple of hours." The clerk passed him a card and a pen. CJ filled out the card and paid him. "Keep the change", he told him. This was the first smile he got from the tall blonde guy. He passed him the key. Once he got inside his room, he closed the curtains and threw his bags on the bed. He first shaved his head and put on the mustache. He then begin putting in the colored contacts. When he put the final trim on the mustache, he stood staring at himself in the mirror. "Yeah that's it CJ. No one will notice me. I am the new and improved CJ with plenty of bread." He took a quick shower and walked back to the front entrance of the motel and asked the clerk to call the number on the card the taxi drive gave him. It didn't take the taxi long before pulling up in the front. "Can you take me to an American car dealership? As in buy car?" He moved his hands as if he was driving. The driver nodded his head and drove him to a dealership. When they pulled up, he saw a Chrysler 300LS sitting in the front. Right away, CJ knew he wanted that car. When the salesman approached him, CJ asked him, "man how much do you want for the 300?" "I am sorry to tell you that, that's my car and I have only had it for one week. It's not for sale." CJ wrote something on a piece of paper and passed it to him and a few minutes later, he was driving off in the black 300. He stopped and did a little more shopping after getting all he wanted for now he headed to the ambassador bridge headed back to Detroit.

Chapter 5

While CJ was driving to Detroit, he daydreamed about how he kidnapped Jada and the way she looked after he gave her the last dose of drugs. She was a beautiful young lady and he really didn't mean to hurt her. He heard a car horn blow and realized that he was weaving a little. He straightened his car. "Well let me pay attention. All I need is an accident plus what happened is water under the bridge". He turned his volume up to Al Green's *Let's Stay Together,* thinking about how he needed his wife and son. He knew quite well Des is not going to turn this money away. It's time for me to show her, he could do better. He still couldn't get out of his mind whether he should tell her about the kidnapping. What if she finds out on her own, then to find out that it was her brother's girl. She might not want to have anything more to do with me. But, I did it for her and Juquan. One thing for sure Maliek will know he shorted me on my money. Oh, there it is a large sign, "welcome to Michigan". It's about time. He hit 94 west and headed into the downtown area of Detroit. Once he saw the Marriot, he decided to pull in. He was dressed in business attire so the clerk thought he was checking in on business. He got away with the "I left my ID in the car" line while he was in Canada. He was able to get a prepaid credit card. Signing his name on the registration card, "do you have access to the internet?" The young attractive clerk responded, "Yes we do. Plus, we have a computer room if you do not have a laptop." "Thank you. I do have my own." CJ said smiling and winking at her. Once he saw her smile back, he knew everything was ok, she was a sight to see only a little heavier than he liked his woman. Plus, his mind was only on one woman, Desarie. He went into his room which was highly decorated in burgundy, beige, and green pastel colors. "This is nice. He plugged up his laptop after everything was up and running. He emailed his wife "I need to see you as soon as possible, the man". After a while, he began pacing the floor, trying to think of what he would say to his wife and what he would do next to Maliek. How dare him, short me on my money. But this will have to do for now. I need my family back. His main concern was to give his wife and son everything that he hasn't since the breakup. Des was fixing Juquan something to eat. He walked up to her, "mommy can I watch the Disney channel?" "Sure anything for my little man. She picked up the remote and turned on the TV and there was a special broadcast airing a Charlie Jackson wanted for kidnapping a federal employee and attempted murder. But when she saw aka roll across the screen, she knew it was her husband. She quickly turned the channel before Juquan could see. "Oh my god. Who in the world did he kidnap?" She thought. She ran over to her computer to turn it on, knowing that if CJ was in trouble, he would try to email her. Of all the begging and trying to get her back, he would always email her. Also, he knew she loved her computer and sending emails. And true enough, she had a new message from him. She emailed him. He quickly responded and told her to come to the Marriot hotel room 405. She called Nana and asked her to watch Juquan for a couple of hours. Nana didn't mind. She loved and adored him as if he was her own. She was one of the women that wanted kids but couldn't conceive. Nana stopped her in

the middle of her asking "Des why are you asking me to watch him? You know to just bring him over. I love to see you get away and have some free time to yourself. I haven't seen you go out since you left that drunkard husband of yours."
"Oh Nana, don't start on him."
"Well, you know how I feel about the way he treated you and that boy. Cursing and acting a fool in front of him all of the time.
"Ok, Ok, Nana. I am on my way." Des hung up and exhaled.
"Juquan, come on honey. Mama has to go out for a while."
"Can I go with you ma?"
"No not this time. But, I will take you somewhere soon."
"Chuckie Cheese", he said looking up at her with his light brown eyes.
"Yes, Chuckie cheese."
"Ok Ma, I'm ready." She left to take him next door. When Nana opened the door Juquan gave her a big hug.
"See you later, Ma."
"Des you know if it's too late when you finish, you can get him tomorrow. You know that boy has to have his rest."
"Alright", Des said. She walked back to her house and got dressed in one of her short skirts with a spaghetti strapped top and some nice Gucci heels. She knew he would be weak to this outfit. She hadn't saw or been with her husband in a long time. Despite of all of their problems, she missed him at times. Only if he could have stopped drinking. He was so caring and generous when he was sober. He was definitely a doctor Jekyll

and Mr. Hyde. After putting on her lip gloss, she headed out to see her estranged husband.

Chapter 6

The next morning Des woke up at Six O'clock. Her first thought was that she had stayed out all night. She had to get home to Juquan. "CJ wake up. I am going to get dressed and get home before Juquan wakes up." While she went into the bathroom to get washed up and dressed, he got out of the bed and took a large sum of money out of his bag. She walked back into where he was just zipping up the bag. "Here", passing her the money. Get my son whatever he wants and spend the rest on yourself.
"This is more than we are going to spend", she said looking at all of the large bills putting them in her purse. She hugged him while kissing him on his lips. "I will see you later today". He walked her to the door and watched her walk to the elevator. Des walked to her car a very happy woman. She couldn't wait to get home and take her little man shopping. Once she drove up, she went inside and re-showered. Picking out a Roca Wear outfit for him, she sung all the way to Nana's house. "Good morning, Chile", Nana said after opening the door. She kissed Nana on the jaw.
"Is he up?"
"Yes, we are in the kitchen about to have breakfast."
"Let me get you dressed, I have a surprise for you today", she said to him.
"Mommy where are we going?"
"I can't tell you. If I do it won't be a surprise will it?
"Ok".
After getting him dressed, she reached in her purse and counted out five one hundred dollar bills and passed them to her grandmother.

"Lord Chile, where did you get this kind of money from?"
"Oh, Nana don't worry about it. Just use it." They both kissed her.
"See you later, Nana", they told her. She stood there smiling at them both.
"Fasten your seatbelt."
"Mommy where are we going?"
"Juquan, stop asking so many questions."
"Alright, Ma."
Des head for Lakeside Mall. She shopped in every kid store in the mall. After shopping for herself, she took him to Chuckie Cheese for an hour. By the time they made it home, Juquan had every name brand outfit and shoes to match, and not to mention the wardrobe she bought for herself. When they made it back to the house, she had a trunk full of bags and half of the back seat. She carried the bags with him trying to help into the house and headed for Nana's house to drop him off again. As soon as Nana opened the door, she let Des know she had been in the window watching her carry the bags.
"Girl you really did some shopping. I saw all of those bags you had. Did you hit the lottery or something?"
"No Ma'am, just say I got a little secret. I'll tell you all about it one day when we are alone", she said winking her eye.
"But enough of that. Here you go." She passed her a bag with a hat in it. Nana loves hats. No one and I mean no one in Detroit could wear hats like her. She peeked in the bad and..."Girl, what are you up to now?" She pulled out the purple felt hat with rhinestones around the side. "This is a beautiful hat. Thank you, honey."

"You are welcome and I have to go. I will see you later. Juquan was so excited about all of the shopping until he didn't even notice his mom leaving. He grabbed Nana's hand trying to explain to her the names of all his new things. Des drove to her hairdresser, Kenya at Cuts and Styles. When she walked in, everyone was looking at her real peculiar. It only let her know one thing. Her name must have come up in one of their conversations. This shop never changes. There were women that came in from all sides of town that knew everyone's business and loved to discuss people like they were in a book club.

"Yes, I am ready for you", Kenya said holding the plastic cape. She sat while fastening the cape around her neck. Kenya couldn't hold it any longer, "girl, I heard about your husband kidnapping that girl". Des gave her a look like I don't know what you are talking about. After Kenya noticed her expression, she changed the subject. Regardless of how nosey Kenya is, she can really lay some hair. After she did the finishing touch, giving her a mirror looking at her twenty seven piece, "girl I love it". Des told her, finally smiling at her appearance. "And, Kenya girl, you really did this coloring." She had it mixed with two different types of blondes. Des paid her and tipped her largely.

"See you later". Des exited the shop. She turned around after and looked back. She could see one lady lifting her dryer in deep conversation. She knew what the subject was about but she really didn't care what they had to say. She was banked. She stopped and had her nails and pedicure done. Now she was ready to see her husband. By the time she arrived at the hotel, CJ had gotten on the computer to process the application for the townhouse. "Baby you are right on time. I have

taken care of everything. All you have to do is go to the office with your ID and SSN card along with your income statement". After telling her the news, he stared up at her, up and down. "You look wonderful".
"So do you."
"Oh you got jokes", he said standing with a towel wrapped around his waist. Des snatched the towel, letting it fall to the floor. She pushed him on the bed and straddled her legs across him. With her free hand, she touched his manhood and he instantly got hard. She didn't have a problem with her underwear because she had on blue thongs. She guided him with her hand until his tip found her entrance. Gliding herself down on him, she rode him until they both came to a peak. After releasing, "so I see you are still trying to get a quickie", teasing her.
"No CJ I was just getting what I really wanted last night but the drinks killed that." They both went into the bathroom to wash themselves, laughing and talking. "We better get to Bloomfield Townhouses before the office closes", he said grabbing her chin, giving her a small peck on her lips. On the way to Bloomfield, he phoned the office on his cell phone. One of the leasing agents told him, "yes we have everything all set up. Just have Mrs. Jackson come in with the proper ID. But, we won't be able to lease to her for six months. I would have to be for one year and the total will be seven thousand, two hundred dollars which needs to be brought in by a money order or cashier check." CJ stopped by the check cashier so she could purchase a money order for the full amount. When DES returned to the car, she fastened her seatbelt looking directly in CJ's eyes, "CJ don't you think you are taking me a little fast?"

"Des, What are you talking about? What is it this time? Are you still upset with me about the kidnapping? I know I did wrong, but could you just put that aside for a while and try to live today for today? We have plenty of money to spend and we don't know what might happen in a spur of a moment, so please stop." He parked in the parking lot. She got out and walked into the business office. It took a little longer than he expected, but when she returned, the deal was settled. CJ pulled out and drove to the back. He drove around following her directions and parked. He walked behind her watching her lavishing legs. "Girl I should but insurance on yours like Tina Turner".

"Oh stop, CJ. Don't start nothing. She opened the door to the townhouse and it was lovely from walking in. There were two bedrooms upstairs with two bathrooms on the inside of the master bedroom. A living room connected to a sunken den with a large kitchen and a half bathroom downstairs. The stairs were twisted in spiral. It also had a basement. "Des this place is so nice, I wish we could all live here and be one big happy family. "CJ, there is no sense in getting all excited. This is only temporary until you can find out what you are going to do with yourself. "Thank you baby", he said kissing her in the mouth. What more could he do for just this moment she had made him very happy. He knew he was wanted but for now, he felt a sense of security.

Chapter 7

(Home Sweet Home)

Jada and Maliek returned to the mansion from the island. The limo drove up in front of the mansion. "Jada how long was you going to let me suffer before you came home?"
"Oh not long at all. I was really missing you and I am sorry for not coming home. I know you went through a lot of trouble decorating for my homecoming. Aaron told me about how beautiful you had things set up. He kissed Jada to stop her from talking.
"We don't need to talk about this anymore. Let's just go in and tell your family the good news". After going inside and telling Ms. James about the engagement, the two of them were tired, so they decided to go upstairs to their room. Aaron left for the club earlier. He decided to bring Regina to the mansion not knowing his sister and her new fiancé was back. Aaron had only been seeing Regina a couple of weeks and on a regular, they seem to be fond of each other. Regina hadn't dated in quite some time, so she was real excited. She took them all over the city. They had dinner, went to movies and hung out at Club Stallion. She really felt special, knowing that Aaron was the owner's future brother-in-law. She walked in the club as if she was a part of the family. Aaron parked the car. "Wow, this place is the bomb", she said opening her door.
"Yeah my sister really have it going on".
"Is your sister here?" she asked as they walked towards the pool area.

"No, I don't think so. At least when I left earlier, she was out of town. But she hasn't been staying here in a few weeks. So Aaron, what am I supposed to wear in the hot tub?"

"Regina, I know this won't be your first time naked. Just get in with your undies on and we will figure out the rest." She stripped and got in. He joined her. They were laughing and talking, splashing water, not realizing what time it was or the volume of the noise they made. Aaron began throwing water. "Stop Aaron", she said splashing back at him. Then all of a sudden she stopped in short. He didn't know what was wrong. She pointed. He turned about and looked at his sister standing there heated with her hands on her hips. "Oh Jada, I didn't know you was going to be here tonight", grabbing his floating boxers.

"I'm sorry Regina. This is my sister, Jada. The one I was telling you about."

"Pleased to meet you, Jada", she said embarrassed. She grabbed her two piece matching set.

"Aaron what do you think that you are doing all out here like you are having a party? What did you think I didn't live here anymore? Please, and you are running around here naked while Mama is here. This is me and Maliek's personal hot tub. No one gets in this tub naked but us. Get dressed and get whatever her name is out of here before you wake Mama up."

"Jada calm down. The way you are talking, you probably have already woke her up."

"I tell you what, Aaron. I am back home now and you can take your little hoochies to the condo. But don't bring them out here unless I know you are." She stormed back into the house. She walked past her mother's room. When she eased the door open

25

thinking she was sleeping. "What have that young man done now, Jada?"

"Nothing Ma, good night". Walking upstairs, she said to herself, "I will deal with him later" then she eased in the bed not disturbing him. Ms. James said "those two never can fool me, I knew Aaron was up to something. God thank you for bringing Jada back home where she belongs."

Chapter 8

The next morning after breakfast since this was Jada's first day back in the mansion, she decided to sit in their large tub that sits inside of their bedroom. She ran the water putting strawberry oils mixed with strawberry bubble bath. She stripped her silk nightie and stepped in. Her whole body longed for a hot bubble bath in this enormous size tub. This tub was triple the size of her tub at the condo. Maliek walked in just as she felt comfortable. "Good morning", he said sitting on the edge of the tub. "Can I join you?" he said kissing her on the lips.
"I don't see why not", she replied.
"I will be right back", he walked out. Jada watched her man, "um, um um, that man". That man Maliek was wearing only silk boxers showing his eight pack and muscular hairy legs. His 6 foot 1 inch frame would make any woman drool. He returned with a tub cushion for her neck while placing it so she could lay back. "It's so good to have you home".
"Yeah, it's good to be home."
Maliek hit the button on the wall radio. It tuned into 92.3fm. Babyface's song *I Give Good Love* was playing. They began to sing to each other. Jada eyes closed as he dropped his boxers to the floor and joined her. He took the sponge and started rubbing her body in circular motions. "Let me see your feet", he said grabbing them one by one kissing them.
"Oh Maliek, you are too much. Baby I have missed you so much."
He said, "is that right?" She stared at him while he massaged her toes singing "soon as I get home from

work". Maliek started kissing her thighs one by one going all the way up until he reached her clitoris. Massaging it with his tongue, he began taking her in to new depths she has never been to releasing all she had. "Oh baby, stop", she cried.

"Ok I'll stop for now" since finding out Jada was carrying his seed, he thought he would take it easier on her. Jada took his sponge and in return bathed her man. All he could do was stare into her beautiful brown eyes. The two continued to caress each other until coming to an agreement to get out. He dried himself. "You hold up, young lady", having her wait. He held the large towel for her to get out. Drying her off as if she was a newborn baby. Then, carrying her over to the bed covering her with the white satin sheets. "Maliek, I don't know what I am going to do with you".

"Just love me. That's all I ask", seeing that she was comfortable. He walked into his walk-in closet to get dressed. She sat up in the bed with the remote to the television watching him as he came out well dressed in a money green colored Gucci suit with green and beige gator shoes. She could smell the scent of his Aramis cologne before he leaned over the bed to kiss her. "I'll see you tonight", he walked out. She said to herself, "I am one lucky woman. I should have known James was Maliek's brother. They are too much alike, fine, smell good, and dress conservatively." He walked back in, "Jada, I forgot to tell you I want you to take it easy and do not go out alone. You know that crazy CJ is still out there running around. I don't trust him, but he sure better be hiding himself well and not let me find him first."

"Maliek, I don't want you looking for him. Let the feds find him", she told him very seriously.

"No Jada, let me handle this. Did the feds find you when he kidnapped you? No, I did. All I am saying is just be careful when I am not around. Remember there are two of you now!"
"Alright baby, I will be careful", she said. He walked out. Jada knew it was time to call her best friend Chi Chi to tell her about the kidnapping. She already knew Chi Chi was going to have a fit being the last to find out. She picked up the phone dialing her home in Atlanta hoping she was not out of town with her new husband. Chi Chi started screaming at the sound of Jada's voice, "girl, it's about time I heard from you. What's going on? How are you doing?"
"Well, I am fine but you are not going to like the latest news. "
"What girl you and Maliek broke up or something?"
"Never", Jada exclaimed. She began to tell her about how CJ kidnapped her and that she was safe and pregnant.
"What! Why didn't anyone call me?"
"Chi Chi, everything happened so fast! One thing led to another."
"Did they catch the trick? I should have had him locked up, when he tried to rape me. I am so sorry. Did he hurt you?"
"Yeah girl, he drugged me but I am ok now. Maliek paid three million to him for my ransom. But Chi Chi, we must move on. Mama and Aaron is here with me."
"Girl, I am leaving today coming to Detroit. I would have been there only if I had known."
"Well let me tell you the other news. Maliek and I are engaged."
"Oh, he finally proposed to you?"
"Yes girl, and we are so happy!"

"I don't doubt that, Jada. Maliek is a good man."
"Anyway, I need you to help me plan my wedding."
"You did not even have to ask me. Look how you helped me with my wedding."
"That's what best friends are for."
"This will work out fine. My husband is doing a lot of baseball practicing this time of year. He is trying to be a good husband. But I asked him about starting a family and he wants to hold off. So, I guess you beat me to the punch. Let me call you back. I am going to call and reserve me a flight." Jada smiled while putting the phone back on the cradle thinking it will be nice to have her friend around. Jada and Chi Chi had been best friends since junior high if CJ wouldn't have tried to rape her, she would still be in Detroit. That really brought a trauma to her life but hopefully she can be happy with this new husband. Jada was excited about her coming so suddenly until she decided to get up and get dressed as soon as she pinned her hair up. Her mom knocked on the door, "come in Ma".
"How are you feeling today, baby", her Mom asked her.
"Ma, I feel like a new woman".
"Good, you are glowing", she said giving her a hug.
"Mama, I really love having you around."
"Yeah, honey but you know I have my own home."
"Benton Harbor is not going anywhere."
"Yeah, Jada but I will not miss the Jazz Festival this year on the lake. Have you heard from your brother today?"
"No not yet, he is probably tired from getting his freak on early this morning".
"Jada", her mother said, "when did you start talking like that?"
"Oh, Mama, I am sorry but my brother he will be here soon. Let's take a walk before we eat lunch."

They walked downstairs out of the mansion when they reached the garden. "This is where I am going to have my wedding".

"That's a good idea. It's beautiful out here".

"Mama, I forgot to tell you Chi Chi will be coming in today."

"Yeah I was going to ask you, have you called her. I can go back home then when you two get together you won't have time for me.

"Mama, I will always have time for you and I want you and Aaron to stay until after the baby is born. I hope that he agrees. He seems to be having the time of his life. Maliek has given him a Benz to drive while he's here and he has plenty of money. I don't think he will be wanting to go anywhere anytime too soon". Sung walked up to where they were standing in the middle of the garden, he grabbed Ms. James' hand. "How are you today", giving Jada a hug. "Are you ladies enjoying this beautiful weather?"

"Yes," Jada answered.

Jada it is good to have you back home again. I heard the good news. It will be nice to have a little one running around here".

"Yes, it will, Sung. I am glad to be back."

"Well, I have prepared a meal with your favorite, shrimp, in it. Now I know why you were craving Shrimp they laughed."

"We will wash our hands and come to the terrace now. I am starving." He walked away. Jada looked at her mother. "Mama, he kissed your hand".

"And, what is that supposed to mean? I am not that old. I still got it girl", putting her hand on her hip, motioning from side to side. They laughed walking back into the mansion. Jada was so happy to have her mom around.

She really didn't want her to leave at all. It took the kidnapping to bring her here for this length of time. Her mother before use to have short visits. They sat on the terrace having lunch. "This is so delicious Mama."
"You like it?"
"Yes, I am enjoying all of the food that he prepared. It takes me away from all the greens and cornbread, Mama. We will never have enough of that. Remember how Daddy use to go to Eau Claire to get all of those fresh greens and I was too young to call myself picking greens?"
"Yeah I really miss your daddy", Ms. James said staring off over the terrace. The phone rang. It was Chi Chi calling to tell Jada that she will arrive at Metro airport at seven o'clock. "I will send you a limo." The two hung up then Jada dialed her brother. All she could hear was loud music. He hollered in the phone, "I am on my way to the mansion" before the phone cut off.
"Your son is on his way", she said to her mother. A few minutes later, he walked up looking all fresh wearing his Sean John jean shorts and a nice t-shirt. "Hey, Ma", he kissed her on the jaw. "Hey Ma Jada", he said laughing soon as he sat down.
"Guess who's coming today", Jada said to him.
"Who"
"Chi Chi"
He smiled looking very devious.
"Don't try it, Aaron"
"What are you talking about, Jada?"
"You know what", Aaron fixed his plate. Jada and her mom smiled at each other watching he amount of food Aaron put on his plate. "You must didn't eat breakfast", Ms. James asked. Aaron continued to eat smiling, "I will see you all later, Mama has to take her a nap".

"Mama you better stop laying down after you eat, you know weight is hard to lose", Jada said.
"Well, I don't care I got to take full advantage of being treated like a queen. You two behave yourselves", she said walking away.

Chapter 9

After Ms. James left. Jada and Aaron sat across the table from each other. "Aaron why did you have that girl in my hot tub naked this morning?"

"Jada that woman was not a hoochie, she is a successful realtor."

"Yeah right. She looked like a stripper, Aaron. I am not mad at you. Just be careful and wear protection. You are new here in this city. I am just concerned."

"Jada you must have forgotten. I am your big brother. I can handle myself. So now my little sister is my Mama?"

"Shut up!" She hit him on his arm. Jada dialed Maliek's number and left him an "I love you" message. Aaron stared in his own thoughts, thinking about the first time Jada brought Chi Chi home to visit their family for spring break and they almost… He quickly snapped back asking Jada "What time did you say Chi Chi would be here?"

"Aaron she will be here at seven o'clock. She is a married woman now."

"Ok Jada, I know." He finished drinking his ice tea. "Jada, let's go into the theater and watch a movie together. When was the last time, we have sat and watched a good movie together?"

"Yeah, it's been some years. Alright, that will work", she said getting up.

"After you, princess Jada". They started out watching *Why Did I Get Married* by the second movie she fell asleep. "Wake up sis, you have missed the movie."

"Why did you let me sleep like that? I told you to put on Ma Dear so I could stay up. No, but you and your

gangster movies." They left and walked to the den where Ms. James was watching Oprah Winfrey. Aaron whispered to Jada. "Please don't make any noise while her favorite show is on".
"Where have you two been?"
"Mama, we was watching a movie but the movie was watching her".
"Yes and Aaron let me sleep through his gangster movie".
"Why didn't you all invite me to the movies? I love movies too. Oh you all probably was watching too much sex stuff".
"No, we didn't ask you because we know you needed your nap", Jada said.
"I was just playing with you all. I only watch certain kinds of movies that was here way before you all was born".
"Mama, Maliek has some old movies that you would enjoy watching. I will take you down there to see the collection when you are ready". After they sat and talking which all of them enjoyed very much when they got together. The time flew by plus it was dinner time Jada couldn't afford to miss any meals. She had to nourish more than herself. This was a lot of getting used to. As soon as they returned to the den, Chi Chi called and told Jada she was pulling through the gates. Jada went out to meet her. Chi Chi stepped out. They hugged each other and smacked each other on both cheeks. "Girl look at you. Aren't you living large?"
"And, you know it", she replied. They walked into the mansion to the den where Ms. James and Aaron sat. "Ms. James", she hugged and kissed her. "Ms. James was just a happy to see her. She has always treated Chi Chi as if she was her very own. Aaron stood with his

arms stretched out. "Don't I get a hug?" She hugged him. "Girl, you look good and you are killing those Apple Bottom jeans!"

"Funny", she said.

"Do you and Jada get tired of wearing stilettos all of the time?"

Chi Chi said, "I do but you know your sister is the Stiletto Queen."

"Look who is talking", Jada said pointing to her shoes. "I see you are still buying every pair you see with blue jean on them!"

"Girl, what floor do you want to sleep on, the first floor down from Mama or the guestroom down from me?"

"I think I want to sleep down from you. Only if you and Maliek promise not to make any unusual noise", she said winking at Jada. "I guess you noticed I am here alone without my husband".

"Girl, trust me, you won't hear a thing. These walls are not like the ones we had in the condo we used to share." The both of them laughed. There were some times back then, when they heard each other. "Aaron will you take Chi Chi's bags to the guest room?"

"Who me", he said laughing. "My pleasure", he said picking up the bags.

"Mama James, I will see you in a little bit. I got to run up and put my things away and call Raymond to let him know I made it safe".

"I will walk with you", Jada said

"You two go ahead I am sure that you have a lot of catching up to do. I will be just fine and I am going to bed when you make it back down, I will see you tomorrow." They walked up the stairs together. As soon as they got in the room, Chi Chi called her husband only to get his voicemail. Jada began to tell her about how CJ kidnapped her and overdosed her with drugs and they both cried. "Jada, I don't know why I didn't file charges on that nut when he tried to rape me. This would have never happened."

"Don't start blaming yourself. This was not your fault."

"No, it's not but I can assure you that, that's when it got started when Maliek fired him for the way he did me".

"Well, girl don't worry about it. They are going to find him".

"Jada, you mean to tell me he is still running around Detroit?"

"Yes, somewhere, but they caught his partner. His name was Doug. Girl, you should have saw who he picked for a partner, a big white guy that sounds like he's black. They caught him at the Athem Hotel partying with a bunch of different women butt naked in the hot tub. Girl, Maliek's boys found him first but the feds followed them and saved his life."

"Well while I am here, I hope they catch that maniac. I don't trust him and neither should you."

"I don't trust him. Remember when I came to help you plan your wedding?"

"Um huh, that same white man followed me to Atlanta."

"Girl, why didn't you say something? He probably followed us everywhere we went. We could have jumped him ourselves."

"Yeah girl, beat the brakes off of him."

"Girl, that's enough about the kidnapping. Tell me what is going on with you and your new husband."

"Marriage is ok. I kind of wish I would have waited a little while. My husband is gone a lot so we don't get a chance to spend a lot of time together. It's baseball, baseball, baseball. But, he is a good provider. We had

our house built in Alpharetta, GA. It's really nice but your mansion makes my house look small. Everyone thinks it's a baby mansion. We have a lot of land surrounding it. I spend a lot of time alone at home so, I have been doing a lot of decorating. Jada, I am tired of that. I need him to spend more time at home."
"Well, all I can tell you is, sit him down and tell him just what you are telling me. And, I hope that things work out. You two seem so happy at the wedding."
"Girl, who don't be happy on their wedding day! So when did Maliek pop the question to you?"
"Girl, when I got out of the hospital, I didn't come here. I went back to my condo. I needed some thinking time. So, when I saw that Maliek was hurt and not running after me, I went to find him and he was on his island. Girl, when I got there in that sexy white two piece with a sheer top, I surprised him. He was laying on the beach and when we did, you know what on the beach, I was at my peak and he asked me." They both laughed.
"Now that's what I am talking about. Put it on him and make him scream marry me, marry me!"
"Girl stop", Jada told her.
"So how do you feel about having a baby?"
"There is nothing to feel. There is nothing I can do about it now and Maliek is so happy."
"Maliek is not the only one happy. I am going to be a godmother."
"Don't you wait too long. Is your husband shooting blanks or what? Regardless of what he feels sometimes things just happen. You don't need his approval to get pregnant."
"Girl, he is talking about waiting five years. But I am on top of him. I have already stopped taking my pills."
"Chi Chi don't force him, if he is not ready."

"Whatever, I know I stay ready. I need a lot of sex."
Jada hit her on her arm. "You are so crazy!"
"Where is Maliek?"
"He finally decided to go back to the club after we returned from our trip. Girl, he shut the whole club down when I got kidnapped."
"No, he didn't...shut down the hottest club in Detroit? He really loves you."
"Yes, he do. I am glad he is gone back to the club. He was smothering me with plenty of love. I have just realized that I'm his real first love and I have never felt this way about anyone."
The two of them talked until they both got sleepy. "We better get some sleep so we can start an early day of planning the wedding", she said hugging her best friend. She walked towards the door. "And, don't think you are going to get out of cooking me some collard greens and fried chicken."
"I miss you, Chi Chi. You really had me spoiled on your Sunday dinners when we didn't eat at Steve's. Good night."

Chapter 10

The next few days Chi Chi and Jada started their wedding planning. They had so much fun together. Since Chi Chi had moved back to Atlanta, Jada had not allowed anyone to become her best friend but her man. One of their college friends recommended Jada to a young wedding planner named Genesis. She had an outstanding background. She coordinated many of weddings. She specialized in high profile couples. All Jada had to do was pick out dresses and colors. Chi Chi and Genesis would take care of the rest. From the beginning, Jada knew Genesis had good taste. Maliek told them to go overboard with this wedding. There was no limit to what it would cost. This would be his first and last wedding. He continued to tell Chi Chi, "don't let my baby overdo herself", then he would laugh and say "my babies." He was one proud father to be. He spent most of his days taking care of his business. He mentioned to Jada, he was going to retire from anything illegal once the baby was born, and we was going to let Ali run the club. His plans were to be a good and model father to his new baby. He was so overjoyed about getting her pregnant so much that he daydreamed about the baby and impregnating her year after year. Sitting at his desk, he thought about so many things including his brother that he just reunited with after ten years. Before he called his brother, he wanted to have a meeting with Ali. He called Ali on his cell phone and asked him to come into his office. Ali came in shortly after. "Have a seat, man." Ali took a seat on the leather sofa across from Maliek's desk. "Ali, I have been doing a lot of thinking lately. I wanted to

get some input from you first. How would you feel, if I let you run the club full time when my baby is born? Before you answer that. I know how loyal you have been to me from day one, protecting me and my establishment. I can trust you with my life. I couldn't think of no one else, I would allow to fill this position when I become a husband and father."
"Man, I don't know what to say. That sounds like a good idea. You know I am the man for the job."
"Ok, well then, you got it and this means you don't need my approval for anything. You will do all of the hiring and firing. Man, I am about to get real legal around here. No more trips or anything. It's me and Jada and our baby. You have looked out for me a many of years. Now it's time for you to get your own life together. Maybe, you will find someone special in your life and settle down, build you a baby mansion and just live, man. You are still young like me and we have made plenty of money. One thing for sure Club Stallion will still bring in a nice sum of money. That's why I invested my money in this business."
"Maliek, I have been thinking about settling down. I have started dating Stan's sister. The young lady that helped us catch one of the kidnappers. And, I want you to meet her."
"I am liking her already."
"Will it be ok to bring her to the wedding?"
"I don't see why not", he replied.
"I expect you to start right after the wedding. You know this club just as well as I do. There are some areas that you don't know about. But, we will discuss that later."
Ali stood up. They shook hands. Ali walked out.
"I guess being Maliek's right hand man is going to pay off finally", he thought.

After Ali left, Maliek called him again. "One more thing, man. I want you to hire as many people as you can to find that CJ. I know he is still out there and probably, no doubt, still have it in for me especially when he only got three million instead of five."

"Yeah, I feel ya. I will get right on it."

Chapter 11

After giving Ali the instructions, Maliek thought about the last time he was with his brother James who is now a preacher and no longer in the game. They made plenty of money together and were very close. What brought on the ten year separation was that James met a young lady named Dawn. They moved in together and fell deeply in love. One night James and Dawn were lying in bed after making love for the second time. His phone rang and it was Maliek telling him that he needed to make an emergency trip to New York. They argued back and forth. James didn't feel like going, but finally agreed to go. Dawn never travelled with him on any of his trips. He never allowed her in any of his business. She was a financial advisor. This time she insisted that she was going with him. They argued back and forth until he gave into her. She was off the next few days from her job so he told her she could go but deep down inside, he didn't want her to go. But, she was not taking no for an answer. The both of them got dressed. This trip was going to be a turn around. Maliek came to pick them up to take them to Metro airport. However, there was a convention in town and the traffic was really bad. Just as Maliek was entering the expressway, he ran a caution light and was hit by a black suburban SUV truck. The impact was so hard that the passenger side of the Benz was crushed which was where Dawn sat. She died instantly on impact. He remembered his brother pulling her from the car and kneeling in the middle of the street with her in his arms. "God take me not her. I am the one who is doing wrong!" He cried uncontrollably holding her limp body.

Her arms dangled to the pavement. He looked at Maliek who barely had a scratch. "Look what you have done! I told you I did not feel like going. No, but you wouldn't let it go. I love her, man. We were going to get married!" He pulled the ring out of his front pocket. He was going to propose to her when they got in the air. He slipped the ring on her finger. "Now she's gone!" The EMIs arrived and put her on a gurney and covered her body. "Maliek, you are on your own man", he screamed. "I am through with you and all of this dirty business!" Maliek tried to console his brother by touching him on his shoulder. "Don't touch me! You get on the plane and do whatever you want. But keep me out of it!" Maliek kept saying to him, "man, I am so sorry". James did not want to hear it. He began walking down the street. Maliek stood there for a long time watching his brother walk out of his life with tears streaming down his face. He blamed himself for what happened and James just disappeared. Seems like he dropped off of the earth, nowhere to be found in the city of Detroit. If I can get my brother back in my life, I know that I can change just like he did. Back in the day, his brother was no joke. He didn't play the radio. Coming out of his thoughts, he dialed the number to the church. Making that trip to church after Jada's kidnapping reunited them together. This was the best feeling Maliek had in a long time. That Sunday walking down the aisle with no one expecting him to come, Jada was in total shock.

"Liberty Cogic, may I help you", the secretary answered.
"Yes, I would like to speak to Rev Turner"
"May I tell him who is calling?"
"Yes, tell him, his brother". She put him on hold with the sound of *The Storm is Over Now* playing. After a

few minutes of listening, he thought about how his father used to play gospel all the time.

"What's up Liekie?" Maliek hadn't been called by that name in a very long time.

"Oh nothing, man. How are you?"

"Fine", James replied.

"Well, I was calling to invite you to dinner tomorrow night."

"Oh, Maliek that sounds good. Where are you living nowadays?" He gave him his address.

"Man are you kidding? I don't believe this. I didn't know that my very own brother lives in that mansion. I used to ride out there just to look. I wanted to know who that brother was that owned that place. What threw me off is it says Montana Estates. When did you change your last name from Turner?"

"A few years back."

"Oh, I see. Now if it would have said Turner Estates, I would have rang the buzzer to be curious." They laughed. "Man you can count on me being there."

"Alright, you can come anytime, but we will start eating around seven o'clock."

"Alright, see you then."

They both hung up feeling excited.

Chapter 12

Maliek called Jada and told her he invited James to dinner and he talked to Ali about what they discussed at the hospital. "Oh that's good news it couldn't have happened at a better time. Mama and Chi Chi are here and they both love to cook soul food. It will be just like the movie."
"Yeah, I bet", he replied this makes me think about when my mother was living. James and I would eat like that all of the time. He is going to have a ball and his favorite meal is peach cobbler so make sure they plan to make that."
"Alright then, I will tell them to make him one to go."
"Alright baby, I love you and I will be home soon."
"I love you too." They hung up.
Aaron took Ms. James and Chi Chi shopping to buy the food. Jada needed a nap so she stayed at the mansion. She gave them five one hundred dollar bills. "What kind of meal are we having", Ms. James said putting the money in her purse.
"Oh, Ma we just want to make sure there is plenty." He drove them to Farmer Jack's grocery store. After getting everything they had on the list, Chi Chi was standing in line and there was a man standing in line who gave her a quick glance and turned his head. She couldn't quite figure it out but something about this man looked familiar to her.
CJ stood in line with a bald head and colored eyes. Chi Chi stared. He was built like CJ, she thought. She never forgot those bow legs. "Are you alright", Aaron asked her.
"Yeah."

"Do you know him or something?"

"No, he just reminds me of somebody." While walking to the car, the flash of CJ came to mind. The way he tried to rape her and she ran out of his house with her clothes torn off, and no shoes. He sure was a monster when he starts drinking but meeting him you would never notice. Chi Chi looked around in the parking lot and saw that man nowhere. CJ sat in his car after putting his hat on. Hitting his steering wheel several times. "Who are those people with her and what is she doing back in Detroit? Only if she was alone, Detroit would for sure have an amber alert." He waited until Aaron pulled off and followed them back to the mansion. He sat in his car from a distance watching them go through the gates. "Well, well, well. This is where they live. Montana Estates. Now I can get the rest of my money. Huh, Ms. Chi Chi. I will give her something to go and tell. This time it will be true and this time he can't fire me. Cops, I don't work for him anymore. I work for me." He pointed to his chest. "I'm the man. Yeah, me!"

Chapter 13

Maliek stood in front of his desk thinking of how his life was changing and the most important thing was that he was in contact with his brother. They shared so many memories together about how they grew up being very close and how they were taught by their parents to do the right thing in life. However, he chose to go out and try new things but it really was time to let go and do the right thing. He closed his briefcase and walked out of his office locking it behind him. When he reached downstairs approaching the main entrance, he ran into Ali. "Man, I am going home", he told him.
"Alright but before you leave walk over to the bar with me. I want you to meet someone. Maliek followed him. Tracey sat there with her lovely legs crossed looking radiant as ever. Ali grabbed her hand, "Maliek this is Tracey, Tracey, this is Maliek, my main man and best friend."
"Nice to meet you, Maliek. This is a nice club."
"Thank you Tracey and nice to meet you. I really appreciate you and your brother's help with my girl's kidnapping. If you ever need anything, just let Ali know."
"Why, thank you. I will keep that in mind. But for now, I have everything I need and more", she said smiling up at Ali. "My baby here takes real good care of me."
"Ok then, if he gets out of hand, make sure you let me know." The two men gave each other the elbow.
"Man, tomorrow night, we are having dinner at the mansion. Why don't you come and bring Tracey. My brother will be there."
"Tracey would you like that?"

"Yeah baby, I would."
"So then, it's settled. You two will be there. Alright man, I'm out of here."
"Let me walk you out." He kissed her and walked with Maliek.
"Man that is a nice girl. I'm happy for you. So that means that you won't be changing women every month now?"
"Yeah Maliek, I guess so. I told you that I am getting into a relationship. If you can do it after all the stars and models you have had so can I."
Goldie drove Maliek's white Jag and stepped out. They shook hands. He also shook Ali's hand. Maliek got in and drove home. When he walked in the mansion everyone was sitting in the den. He peeked his head around the doorway. "Oh there you are", Jada said. He walked in. "What, did I miss something?"
"No, we were just talking about the wedding." He gave Chi Chi a hug.
"I am glad you could make it now Jada you have your best friend and what's the other lady's name? Genesis, so don't overdo yourself. Why we are talking, call her up and ask her to come to the dinner tomorrow so that I can discuss the security for the wedding."
"What's up Aaron", he gave him some dap and turned to kiss Ms. James on the cheek. He kissed Jada until Aaron cleared his throat. "Hey, hey save some of that for the wedding." Everyone started laughing.
"I'm going upstairs to take a shower and lay down for a while. Jada don't be too long." She smiled at him. He winked at the love of his life while walking out. When Jada finally made it upstairs, Maliek was sound asleep. She crawled in bed and watched him rubbing her

stomach. "Your daddy is the best." Ms. James went to bed leaving Aaron and Chi Chi talking about old times.

Chapter 14

After CJ left the mansion, he drove to his townhouse. He didn't notice Desarie's car outside. Once inside, he hear running water upstairs. "Who in the…" He walked back to the door to see if he saw any unfamiliar cars. He sat the bags down and pulled out his thirty-eight special and walked up the stairs with his feet barely touching. He looked around his room, then walking to the bathroom, he pointed his gun straight at his wife. She grabbed her chest. "CJ, what are you doing?" The scare of the gun made her turn the shower off. "What are you going to shoot me?" He tucked the gun in his pants. "No baby, I just didn't know who was up here."

"You must have forgotten that I have keys to this house", she said grabbing the towel, wrapping it around her still shaking from the scare.

"Come here." He grabbed her. "I didn't mean to frighten you. Let me make you feel better." He grabbed the towel and let it fall to the floor. She grabbed his belt and started to unbuckle it seeing that his manhood stood in full attention. He picked her up and carried her to the king size blown up air mattress taking the remainder of his clothing off in a matter of seconds. He climbed on top of her kissing her passionately while he massaged her breasts. Des wrapped her arms around his neck. He continued to kiss her all the way down to her navel then putting her legs on his shoulders entering her with a deep thrust.

"Oh CJ, Ah" she screamed as he thrusted in and out of her womb. Sweat began to pop on his forehead with each stroke. The room got heated. He stopped and flipped her over and entered her from the back holding her shoulders. "Des, this is so good, I missed you baby." "I miss you too", she said in a seductive tone. He positioned himself upward and started slapping her on her buttocks. "That's it, baby", he said. They both began to have an ultimate release, "Ohhhhhhhh, CJ" she screamed. Both of their bodies began to have convulsions. He held himself still while releasing what little he had left. He fell on the side of her. She turned over. "CJ, you haven't made love to me like that since the night we were married." He laid breathing hard with a flash of Chi Chi going across his mind thinking of how we wanted to do her the same way. Seeing her today made him want her even more sexually. He looked at his wife pretending she was Chi Chi. They both were so exhausted that they fell asleep listening to each other breathe. They slept so hard until the next morning at seven o'clock. When she woke up, "CJ wake up, I caught a cab here last night because I thought it was about time that you see Juquan. So, I need to drive your car today to pick him up and we all can go somewhere together."

"Ok baby, whatever you want to do." She got up and showered and put on the clothes she brought with her. She gave it to him as usual wearing a Gucci skirt and top with Gucci shoes. He looked at her as she got dressed. "Um, um, um", he said. "You hurry up and get back here." She grabbed his keys and left. She went straight to Nana's house. When she opened the door, "good morning, Nana."

"He's woke."

"Mommy, Mommy", he said walking towards her.

"Hey baby." She got him dressed in the outfit that she bought the night before. "Nana you don't know how much I appreciate you."

"Don't worry about it Chile. You two are the only children that I have."

"Let's go, Tiger."

"Mommy where are we going?"

"I have a surprise for you."

She reached in her Gucci purse and pulled out two hundred dollars. "Here Nana."

"Girl, I told you, you don't have to pay me for keeping my boy. He is great company to me."

"Nana, I know but if I have it then you have it." They both kissed her on the cheeks at the same time giving her a loved and caring feeling within. When they got outside, "Ma whose car is this? We have a new car", he said excitedly. Desarie just shook her head at her son unlocking the door. They got in and drove to Bloomfield townhouses. She called CJ on her cell phone. "Come on out. We are outside."

"Ok", he replied. When Juquan saw who was coming outside, he unfastened his seatbelt, opened his door, and ran to his father. "Daddy, Daddy!" He ran straight into his out stretched arms. They embraced each other for more than three minutes CJ felt the love his son had for him. "Where have you been Daddy", Juquan asked him with his beautiful brown eyes looking into his dad's eyes. "Well Daddy has been on a little vacation."

"Well, why didn't you take me and ma?"

"Well, I can't tell you right now but I am here now." Des sat in the car and watched father and son reunion. They finally got in the car after Juquan's twenty questions. "Where would you like to go young man", CJ asked him.

"To the carnival." Des drove to the carnival on twelve mile. They had so much fun. It was just like being a family again. Little did he know his father was a very wanted man and this will come to an end soon. CJ had made up in his mind that he was going to enjoy every moment he has with his wife and son. Every minute counts after they left the carnival. They took him to the park but Juquan wanted to go back to the carnival and they gave him his wishes.

Chapter 15
(Reunion time)

Chi Chi and Ms. James started cooking early and Sung was right beside them. He was enjoying learning how to cook soul food. He knew a little about soul food but this was on hand experience. Now being a top chef and picking this up, would make him even a better cook.

Everyone was dressed and ready for this event. They laid the enormous sized dining room table out. It was decorated with a white lace table with white and red candles in gold candle holders surrounding the silk plant centerpiece. The table was twenty five feet long and ten inches wide with a spread of collard greens, corn bread, fried chicken, fried corn, mac and cheese, string beans with neck bones and potatoes, baked turkey necks, potato salad, and for desert lemon cake, and peach cobbler. Maliek walked in as they were putting the food on the table. "You all have really out done yourselves." He grabbed a napkin and picked up a chicken wing. "Sung did you learn a lot today?"
"Yes, matter of fact, I did. I have it going on now." Maliek laughed. This was more than just a dinner to him. It was a reunion that was long overdue with his brother. Time was growing near for the guests to arrive. Jada, Aaron, Chi Chi, and mom waited in the den. Maliek walked outside to greet Ali and Tracey. They parked and got out wearing matching Emce blue jean suits. Maliek's phone rang again. It was his

brother Rev James Turner III. "Hey brother, I am at your gate. Maliek gave him the gate code. "Now keep that in your head. You can come and go as you please."

"I will. I am definitely going to take advantage of this basketball court, whipping you." He drove through in his 2007 seven series Benz, all grey. He parked and got out, decked out in a royal blue long jacket suit with shoes to match. His hair was freshly cut exposing the natural waves. This was one fine brother. As he closed his door. "Man, did you come to preach? You look just like Dad in that suit."

"I should turn this place into my church. It's twice as large as my church. "They hugged each other and shook hands. He put his arm around his shoulder. "Man, let me show you around." They walked through the nine bedroom mansion with a huge swimming pool, sauna, tennis court, basketball court, and mini football field. "Man, this place is out of sight", leaving the guest houses. "You have so much here, you never have to leave", James said.

"Yeah James, that's about the size of it. I have made up in mind to retire from all wrong doings. And guess what? I am going to be a father."

"What man you mean, I am going to be an uncle?"

"Yes, you are and I want to ask you will you be my best man in my wedding?"

"You know I am all for that, man. That is the best news that I have heard in a long time. Congratulations, man. Now you even have a good woman one that loves you I will be glad to be your best man and I will have one of my associate ministers to perform the ceremony."

"Thanks man, this really means a lot for me." They walked to the dining room where everyone was waiting. Ali stood up to greet James with a hand shake. "This is my right hand man", Maliek said.

"Well, I finally get to meet Maliek's brother after all of these years. James walked over and kissed Moms on the cheeks.

"It's good to see you again."

"You too, Rev." After meeting everyone, he sat down. James blessed the food. "Lord, thank you for everyone that is present. Lord, thank you for me and my brother reuniting. Bless this food for the nourishment of our bodies, Amen." They all fixed their plates. Sung came to the doorway. "Jada, someone is here to see you." Jada got up and went to the front entrance. It was Genesis. "Come on in, we have just blessed the food. Come on in and join us." They walked back into the dining room. Genesis was a very pretty young lady and well dressed. Jada introduced her everyone. "This is my wedding planner." James and Aaron's eyes were glued on her. She sat by James and there was something between them. Neither knew what, but it was something that made Chi Chi hit Jada on the arm whispering, "girl, Maliek's brother is so fine. You didn't tell me that. I wish I was single." Jada held her napkin to her mouth and played it off with a smirk grabbing her glass of water. James finally spoke up. "I want to know who cooked all of this delicious food?" Jada was the first to speak. "My mom and best friend along with Sung our personal chef." He looked at Chi Chi. "Well young lady, your husband must be a happy man."

"We don't get to eat a lot of this kind of food often. He plays pro baseball but that don't stop him on holidays."

"Is that right?" He replied with a smile.

They all ate until they couldn't eat anymore. When they finished, they walked into the large family room. Maliek said, "everyone my brother has agreed to be my best man in the wedding." Everyone started clapping. They discussed the wedding and Maliek told Genesis about his plans for security for the day of the wedding. Genesis sat by the Rev and sparks were flying everywhere. He finally asked her, "are you married?"

"No I'm not." I was engaged and I lost my fiancé a year after he got drafted to the NBA league. The day before the wedding, he had a tragic accident. "Well are you married", she asked him.

"No, not at this time. I kind of lost someone the same way you did. Now, I am just waiting on God. I'm sure no doubt, he will send me the right one at the right time. Why don't you visit my church sometime?"

"I will keep that in mind."

The entire evening went very well and James was the first to say he had to leave. Maliek and Ali walked him to his car. "I guess, I will be seeing you brothers at church sometime. You know even when we are doing wrong, we have to give God some time."

"Yeah you are right", Ali spoke.

"I'll be right back", Maliek said walking back into the mansion. He walked back out with a peach cobbler in his hand. "Here man, I almost forgot your surprise. This was especially made for you." You should have seen the look on his face when Maliek gave him the pan. "Man, I am going to have a good time with this tonight! We got to start having dinners like this often." He got in his car and rolled his window down. "Man, I know your gate code now so don't be surprised when you see me out on the court bouncing the ball."

Ali said, "did he say what I think he said?"

"Yeah, I think I heard the same thing", Maliek said looking at them both.

"Just because I am a preacher don't get it twisted, remember I know every kind of game it is to play and I will run circles around you both", he exclaimed.

"We can go now", Maliek said.

"Yeah sure can", Ali commented.

"You fellers calm down. I got a meeting. What about Saturday afternoon?"

"Ok, bet", Maliek said. They all shook hands and James drove off. They stood and watched him go all the way through the gates. "Man, I like your brother already. He is a cool dude."

"Yeah, he has always been and you think you don't play when you get mad? Well, you don't have anything on him when someone rubs him the wrong way. When my brother was in the game with me, no one and I mean no one wanted to piss him off, not even me." Jada and the girls sat and listened to a lesson on how to be a good wife from Ms. James. They were cracking up. Tracey and Genesis seem to fit right in. They were having the time of their lives. Genesis felt real comfortable with her new clients. She felt apart of them from the beginning. Aaron was on the phone trying to call Regina. He told Jada, he was the only one that didn't have a date. "This wasn't a dating thing, Aaron. Just a family dinner. Why do you always have to have someone?"

"You know me." After Maliek and Ali returned Chi Chi began to tell them about when they went shopping for the food, she saw a man that could have been CJ. He just had a bald head and colored eyes. "I'm glad you told us. There is a possibility that he could have tried to disguise himself." Ali got instantly mad. "Well, Tracey and I are going to the club." We will see you all later." Jada walked with Tracey while Maliek and Ali stood having a private conversation walking behind then. "Girl, I had a good time. "

"I am glad you did. You are with Ali now. You are just like family." Tracey hugged her. "Girl, your house is so tight. I have never seen anything like this. This is the first mansion I have ever seen besides the ones I see in magazines and on television."

"Thank you, girl. I am sure Ali will bring you back sometime." He walked up. "Baby are you ready?" He said before opening her door. Maliek told Jada. "Baby did you see that boy is serious."

"I see he is. I am happy for him. He deserves someone now that I have you tied up all of the time." They laughed going back into the mansion. They walked in to tell Ms. James, Chi Chi and Aaron goodnight before going to their bedroom. Ms. James was tired so she went to bed. Chi Chi started to go upstairs. Aaron interrupted her. "I know you aren't sleepy this early. Let's hang out a little while."

"No I am not sleepy but I have to go up and call my husband. I will be back down."

"Just meet me at the pool. Let's take a dip and enjoy this nice weather. Maybe have a drink."

"Ok that sounds good." She went upstairs to call her husband. She didn't get an answer. She called several times leaving him a message. "Ray honey, give me a call. I want to talk to you. Call me back. I will be home in a few days. I miss you." She hung up and walked downstairs on to the pool area. Aaron was just walking out of the room that Maliek kept all kinds of swimwear, goggles, and floats. He had taken a bottle of Moet out of the fridge. There was a mini bar inside of the room. He sat on the edge of the pool while she went in to get changed into a swimsuit. Walking out wearing a lime green yellow and orange two piece suit. He watched her walk to the diving board. Her waist couldn't be any more than nineteen inches and her curves showed before she dived of the diving board.

"I need to burn off some of that food we ate tonight", she said. As soon as she came up for air, "what are you waiting on?" He dived into the pool. They started racing back and forth as if they were in the junior Olympics. She stopped at one end. He kept going until he realized she had stopped. "That's cheating", he said. She burst out laughing. She floated to the steps with her back turned. He swam until he reached the back of her legs which caused her to stumble. He reached and grabbed her so that she wouldn't fall picking her up from the waist. They were standing close enough for her to feel and see his shaft sticking straight out. It startled her because it was between her legs. "I'm sorry", he said. "Are you alright?" He grabbed her face. She snatched his hand away from her face and got out of the pool, grabbed a towel and left. He stood there saying, "what did I do", looking down at himself. "Oh", he rubbed himself saying, "look what you did...scared her off." After drinking, he showered and got dressed heading for the club. He was in heat now. Everyone at the club had gotten used to seeing him almost every night. He had access to every part of the club. He could be VIP or laid back. It didn't matter. The women were definitely on him. He was sitting at the bar when Regina walked up. "Oh so you can't return any of my calls?"

"No, Regina. I can say that for you, I tried to call you earlier to see if you wanted to go tonight. I have been with my family all day." She sat next to him and softened up some.

"Let's have a couple of drinks and get out of here."

"You down for that", he asked.

"Yeah, I guess", she said knowing she wanted some more of Aaron for the night that they spent together.

Chapter 16

After a full day of having fun at the carnival and shopping, Juquan was so tired that he stretched out on the back seat while CJ drove them home. "I really enjoyed spending the day with you and my son", he said grabbing her left hand.

"Yeah, we had a good time too. It was just like old times", she replied. She looked in the back seat and saw that Juquan was sound asleep before asking, "have you thought about turning yourself in and getting a good attorney to represent you? I am sure you won't get that much time. It was just a kidnapping and no one was hurt too bad."

"Des that is easy for you to say. You have never been locked up a day in your life. I don't plan on spending half of my life behind bars either."

"I was just making a statement. You don't have to get all upset about it."

"Well, forget about it. I will figure out something".

"CJ, I told you I am not going to drag our son around the country looking behind our backs every five minutes."

"Ok Des, that's enough. This is not the right time to be talking about this."

"Ok but you need to make the right decision soon."

"Des, don't worry about it. I want you to come to the townhouse early tomorrow so I can take you to trade your car in for a new one."

"Ok you know I will be there with bells on."

He drove in the driveway. "You want me to carry him in?"

"No, I got him", she kissed him and they said their goodnights.

When he drove off, he decided to drive over to Jada's condo. He saw the same Benz parked in the driveway that he saw at the grocery store. He drove around the corner and parked. He got out and walked around the back in view of the patio. He looked through the half pulled blinds and saw a woman that he didn't recognize. However, he could see that she was with the same man he saw with Chi Chi at the store shopping. He moved closer, this time getting his eyes full of the young lady's mouth on the guy's manhood. He heard a lot of moans and groans. He watched them have wild sex for a while then he decided to leave. There is no sense in making any dumb mistakes. He walked back to his Chrysler 300 very confused about who the two people were in the condo. He wished the lady would have been Chi Chi. He would have done away with the strange man and gave Chi Chi the sex of her life making her pay for getting him fired from the club and now that he is on the run that would have been perfect if only it would have been true. He continued driving towards Bloomfield until he saw the first liquor store. He went in to buy him a bottle of Jack Daniels. When he got back to the car, he popped the top on the liquor and took a swallow. "Now that's what I am talking about." He was already beginning to feel better. He got home and drank until he fell asleep.

Chapter 17

Jada woke up to find out that Maliek had not left for work. "Honey why are you still here?" He kissed her. "You must have forgotten that we have an appointment today for an ultrasound. And, I know that you didn't think I would put my club or business before this."

"Oh Maliek, I almost forgot about my appointment."

"Ok, the sooner you get dressed and eat something, we can be on our way." While Jada got dressed, Maliek called and told Ali to start working on that phone book he found in CJ's house. "Alright, man I thought about the same thing. I will call you later." They hung up.

Jada and Maliek drove to her doctor's office. She checked in with the receptionist and sat beside Maliek. They held hands looking at each other with excitement. This was something new for the both. "Ms. James, please step into examination room three." They walked in hand-in-hand. Maliek was going all the way after she changed. "Dr. Schram will be with you shortly", the nurse told them. She looked at Maliek as if she wanted him to leave. "Why you looking like that?" She said in a playful tone. "Jada, do you remember that night on the beach?" They reminisced, feeling the heat from that day. The two of them were so happy and full of life. The doctor and nurse returned. "Are you sure you are comfortable with the father in the room while I examine you?"

"Yes, Doc. He won't leave if we asked him to." They all laughed. They proceeded with the exam while Maliek asked about a midwife. "I would like to have him born at home." Jada raised up. "What makes you think it's a boy?"

"I just know it is", he said smiling.

"Well, my wife is a midwife. If you would like her to deliver at home, she is the one. You can let me know a little further down the road. It is yet early, but I do recommend that you two take Lamaze classes. Once they put the cold cream on her belly, they hooked her up to the ultrasound machine. He described every part of the baby to them both while their eyes lit up with joy. "Would you like to know the sex of the baby?" They both decided that they wanted to wait. "I don't want him filling the mansion with all that baby stuff yet", Jada said. The exam and ultrasound went well. The doctor told them to look to birth a healthy and normal baby. "Why thank you, Doc", Maliek said shaking his hand. He wrote her a prescription for prenatal vitamins and iron pills. He also gave them the information on where they could register for Lamaze classes. After Jada got dressed, Maliek walked out with the picture of the ultrasound in his hand. The proud father. "Can I see the picture?" She asked him.

"No, not yet", he said playing. He then passed her the picture. "Thank you. I can see now how you are going to act when the baby gets here." He opened the door for her and walked to get in. "Where would you like to each lunch?" He asked her knowing the answer already. "Don't tell me, Red Lobster."

"Yes, Maliek. How did you know?"

"I know you want seafood almost everyday." He headed in the direction of the restaurant, noticing her staring out of the window in deep thought. "What's on your mind?" He asked her. "How would you feel if I went back to work at the bank?"

He hit the brakes. "Did I hear you right? Just tell me you are having a reaction from the ultrasound." He pulled over to the side of the road. "Jada, I know I didn't hear you say to wanted to go back to the bank where you got kidnapped from. If you did, that's out of the question."

"Maliek I was just thinking about it. I miss my job and before I got kidnapped, I got that new position with that large laid out office. I didn't even get a chance to be a senior banker."

"Jada you can be a banker at home. You can set yourself up to work from the mansion. We have plenty of room to make you an office. But, going back downtown is out of the question."

"Maliek, it won't be the same as going to work all day away from the mansion. I know you don't want me to work but..." He cut her off. "But no, I can't afford to let anything happen to you or my baby. And that CJ is still running around out there like a loose cannon."

"Maliek, I am not going to keep hibernating from him all of my life." The conversation got a little intense. By the time they made it to Red Lobster, she changed her mind. "I want to go home", she said looking out of the window in silence. It has been a long time since they had any kind of disagreement or any type of argument. When they drove in front of the mansion, he got out to open her door and kissed her on the lips. She said "think about it."

"I already have", he replied walking back to the drive side, getting in the car. All the way to the club Maliek thought, "She must be losing her mind. I will not let her go back to the bank not now not ever."

Chapter 18

Ali pulled out the address book he had taken from CJ's house the day they found Doug in the hotel. He begin browsing through it trying to find leads to where CJ might be. There were a lot of numbers and only about ten numbers without addresses and ten addresses without numbers. Two in Florida and some in New Jersey. "Ok CJ, it's time for me to hunt you down. So come from under your little rock." He stuck the book in his pocket and left the club. He drove home to change cars. When he reached his apartment home, he jumped in his Chevy Tahoe in case it was a shoot out. Every time, he looked at the display of cars Maliek had blessed him with over the years, he thought, "he is one of a kind". He drove to one of the addresses. There were two middle aged men sitting on the porch talking. He interrupted their conversation with a "hello, how are you doing?" One spoke and the other one stood up with his hands in his pockets. "What do you want?"

"I want to know if either of you have seen CJ."

"Why", the man answered.

"Man, I didn't come here for any problems. But we can have some if you make it like that", Ali said exposing his holster that carried his gun.

"Shut up", the man sitting said, "before you get someone hurt. Naw man, we haven't saw CJ in a while.

We used to be drinking buddies some years ago. What's wrong with him", he asked.

"Nothing is wrong with him, but I need to find him." Ali pulled out a card with his cell number on it and passed it to the man. "If you see him, don't say anything to him. Just give me a call and I will have a reward for you." They both said in unison, "we will help look for him if money is involved." Ali didn't comment, he walked back to his truck and pulled off. He pulled over and got his map out . Some of the streets he saw in the book, he never heard of in all of the years living in Detroit. By the time, he reached the fifth house, he was getting frustrated. He made several phone calls to people he knew in Florida and Jersey to give them the information. They told him that they would surely check into if a CJ was running around in their town. Ali had connections everywhere. One thing for sure, CJ kidnapped the wrong girl. Maliek was seriously going to find him if he was anywhere to be found. Ali drove all over Detroit putting out the same word the way he did during the kidnapping. When money is involved, someone will always talk.

Chapter 19

Stan and Tracey

The money that Stan and Tracey got from Maliek for their information on one of the kidnappers (Doug) was enough to move them into a nicer apartment. Tracey had really good taste. She had no problem helping her brother who had been out of work for a while. She took four thousand dollars, furnished and made the place real nice. Stan stood in the middle of the floor. She did the whole apartment in beige and rust. "Sis you need to go in to interior decorating."

"Well you know Stan, I've been thinking about the same thing lately and my life is changing since I have started dating Ali."

"You know girl, Mama would have been real proud of you right now." The two of them grew up in the hood on Lemay. They had a hustling mother. She got in and never got out alive. She hustled until one day she got robbed and they didn't only take the money but took her life. No matter what she did, she took very good care of her children. They didn't want for anything. Tracey learned to dance by watching her mother. Her mother knew every way there was to making money. She got it one way or the other. This new apartment was a new beginning for them both. "Stan, I think I am going to enroll in school in the fall."

"Sis that is so good and I am going to try to find me another job so I can help you. And, I am sure that your new man will also. Do Ali know you are still dancing?"

"No, not really. I think I better tell him. That is why I finally decided to invite to our new place tonight."

"That sounds like a hint for me to go out for the night." She hit him on the arm and laughed. "Stan, I didn't say that."

"You didn't have to. Remember, I am your big brother. I know you very well. But I had planned on going out anyway Sis. I really want to tell you that I really appreciate how you handle our household and making sure we have everything. I love you for that. What would I do without you? You turned out to be a very responsible young lady." He gave his sister a hug as if it was the last one. Stan went in to shower and get dressed while Tracey danced around putting the finishing touch on the tables listening to 92.3 fm. When Stan stepped out he didn't look the same as when he went in. He wore a two piece linen suit with Gators. "Wow, Stanley, you must be looking for another Queen as you call them. Why are you leaving so early in the day? Ali won't be here until later."

"Sis, I got to get out and get my hustle on before going to the club. Plus I know you want to get all sexy up before he gets here. I will just get out of your way."

"Ok, if you insist."

"I will see you later. Maybe in the morning, it all depends on who I might run into tonight."

"Alright, don't do nothing I won't do." Stan left.

Tracey phoned Ali. "Baby I hope you didn't think I wanted to meet you at your house. I have a surprise for you. Come to our new apartment."

"Alright, I will see you in a couple of hours", he said. Ali was waiting for her to invite him, ever since they moved in but he didn't pressure her. She was coming to his place and meeting him at the club and that was fine with him. He felt the only way you can have a good relationships is to let a woman have her freedom and don't pressure her into nothing. They hung up and everything was all set. It was her and Ali tonight.

Chapter 20

Desarie took Juquan to Nana's house and drove to Bloomfield on her way. She had all sorts of thoughts going through her mind. She wanted to go earlier but she thought she would give CJ a little time. Plus, he must remember, she cannot just run out on Juquan. He wants to ask all kinds of questions and she has to take care of him first. Now that he has seen his dad, he really has a lot of questions. Some she can't answer. Some she can. She parked the car and went in. Once inside, she was glad she gave him time. He was just getting in the shower. She noticed the Jack Daniels bottle and figured out why. "Oh, he has started drinking heavy again." Right way, she knew what kind of mood he would be in. She hollered up the stairs. "Honey, I am downstairs waiting for you." She heard the water stop. "I will be down in a minute." He got dressed and came down. "I thought I told you to come early this morning, Des." She didn't say anything. She knew where the conversation would end up. "I said I was looking for you this morning."

"CJ, I heard you. I don't feel like I need to answer you. I can see you had one of those nights."

"What nights? I only had a drink or two." He responded aggressively. She picked up the bottle. "This don't look like two drinks to me. Who are you trying to convince", she said. "Alright, Alright so I had some drinks. Don't start that nagging. I am not in the mood."

That just did it. She put her Coach bag on her shoulder, "I don't have to stay here and let you talk to me like I am your child. I am outta here." She stormed out of the door and slammed it so hard that one of his new pictures fell off the wall. He ran out the door behind her, but she was just pulling off. He got in his car and went behind her. After he got to the second light, he would see that the police had her pulled over. He drove pass real slow. "I should shoot him for stopping my wife. Wow, just think I could have been in the car with her. She know not to do anything wrong in this neck of the woods. This time of the month, he must be trying to meet his quota. I better be extra careful driving out here", he said. He pulled into the gas station right before the expressway and waited for her. She drove in when she saw him a few minutes later driving up beside him rolling down her window. "Did you have enough money to pay for that ticket on the scene?"

"Yes, I did. But, he had a smart mouth and I pissed him off."

"What did you say, Des?"

"I got smart back at him. I don't have any warrants. I can say what I want to and he is not going to talk to me any kind of way because he has a badge."

"Des, I am sorry. Now can we start this day over?"

"Well, follow me." He took the expressway west to 10. He made so many turns but Des kept up with him. They ended up on Boulevard. "I guess he knew what he was doing all the time. " He pulled into a Cadillac dealership. Des looked around while CJ talked to the salesman. He called her, "come here baby. This is your new car. It was a Cadillac SIS, all black. She jumped in the car with CJ as they rode to the bank with CJ to get a cashier's check. When they returned, he paid cash and the salesman hooked her up with insurance through the dealership for one year. What more could a girl ask for. She hugged and kissed him passionately while they leaned up against her new car. Regardless of how CJ was at times, he tried his best to make Des happy. They got in their cars and drove off.

Chapter 21

Jada walked in the mansion after Maliek dropped her off. Mom and Chi Chi were sitting on the terrace enjoying the lovely view. They watched a family of blue birds make a nest in one of the large oak trees that surrounded the grounds. "Hello you two", she flopped in the chair beside her mother. "What's wrong", her mother asked after seeing the expression on her face. "Oh nothing to worry yourself about, Ma. Just a little disagreement Maliek and I had on the way home." "You want to talk about it?" Chi Chi asked.

"No not really. But I see you all really want to know. I want to go back to work and Maliek is totally against it."

"Girl are you talking out of your head?"

"I don't think so either not until the baby is born", her mother mentioned.

"Girl that crazy man CJ is still on the loose. That is not a good idea", Chi Chi commented.

"I should have known that everyone would agree with him no matter what I want to do."

"No, sweetheart, Mama is not taking anyone's side. She only wants what's best for you."

"Mama, Ok look at your grandbaby", she passed her the picture of the ultrasound.

"Lord this modern technology. You can see the child before it's born. I wish your father were here to see this. He would be tickled to death."

"I wish Daddy was here too. I believe he is somewhere looking down and if he was here, he would talk to you all until yall would agree on me making my own decisions."

"Girl, you are definitely right. He let you have your way. You had this look that you used to give him and no matter what it was, he would do it or make sure it was done. And, he dared me to say anything. But, now he's gone and you have to listen at me." That made her laugh.

"Jada, Genesis will be here today with some fabric for the bridesmaid's dresses and the portfolio of the different styles of gowns made by Vera Wang for you to choose from."

"Ok girl, I am ready. I will see you all later, I have some calls to make. Plus, I am still working on your invitations." Again, she kissed Mrs. James on the cheek and left. "That girl have worked her butt off for this wedding, Jada and she is truly what you call a friend. She told me that you are flying most of your college friends in and their husbands."

"Yes Ma, we are. We are doing it real big."

"That's good. I am happy for you and I love my new son. He is so good to you and he is going to make a wonderful father and husband. I hope that Chi Chi's husband comes around. She want a child and he shouldn't make her wait. Chi Chi came back in to ask Jada a question about the list. Aaron walked up wearing his Roca Wear shorts and top with matching gym shoes looking real fresh. They all turned and stared at him. "What", he said raising both hands. Jada shook her head. "Hey, party animal".

"Jada don't start that", he replied. "So what yall talking about? Don't tell me, the wedding?" "Matter of fact since that is the discussion, Sis can I bring a guest to the wedding?"

"Yeah, Aaron I don't see a reason why you can't." Chi Chi rolled her eyes and Mrs. James caught her eye. Jada noticed it also and changed the subject. "Why don't we go to the club tonight and hang out? We haven't taken Chi Chi out since she's been here. You don't mind do you, Mama?"

"No girl, I find plenty to do when you all are not here." Aaron spoke up. "So tell me what are you doing? Uh huh, don't let me find out."

"Wouldn't you like to know? I will keep that to myself."

"Boy, leave Mama alone. Just worry about all of those hoochies you meet all up in the club."

"Don't hate the Big D loves me. I will meet you all. I am going to hit lakeside mall for awhile. "

"You and who?" Jada asked him. "Don't worry about that. You have enough to worry about with the wedding."

"Aaron you sure are learning to get around Detroit.
"Chi Chi, you and Jada stop drinking that haterate juice. I will see you all later."

"Jada, I want you to take me to the theater and show me the old movies." I plan to ask Sung to join me in watching movies tonight."

"Ok Ma, I don't have time to discuss this with you right now." She grabbed her mother's hand. Chi Chi walked behind them going to the theater.

Chapter 22

Jada walked into the guest room where Chi Chi slept. She was talking on the phone. She held her finger up to motion for her to wait a minute. After hanging up the phone from her husband, Jada pulled out the surprise she had waiting for her. It was a Chanel dress. One that she bought from one of the boutiques when she and Maliek flew to Paris. "Put this on, girl. I have one similar. Go ahead and start getting dressed. I am going to get into the shower. We will leave in about", she glanced down at her Rolex watch, "one hour and fifteen minutes."

"Girl what is the fifteen minutes for?"

"What do you think, my lips? You know how I do it when I am stepping out." Jada left the room with her hands on her hips looking back at Chi Chi. Once they got dressed, they met downstairs. Once looking at each other, "girl, Maliek is going to make you sit in his office all night with that dress on, fitting like that!" Both of them looked outstanding. Jada's dress was teal green and Chi Chi's dress was yellow and out of all of the Chanel dresses available in the US, none could top this Paris original. This moment gave Jada a flash back of how she met Maliek. She and Chi Chi saw him in a magazine ad promoting his new club. She knew then, she wanted him. After going to the club the first night, he watched her on his security monitor and had to have her. He watched her all night without formally meeting her. It wasn't until the following week when she met him in person. She never will forget the way he looked after sending his limo to pick her up for dinner. When the elevator swung open, he stood there in his 6ft 1 inch fine frame. She thought she had died and went to heaven. "Jada, Jada", Chi Chi called. "Girl what are you thinking about?

"You won't believe me if I told you. I was thinking about the first time we went to Club Stallion."

"Yes, I will believe you and how can I forget. That's when I met CJ and I thought he was this fine intelligent bartender until I went to his house and he had a few drinks."

"Let's not talk about that. But, let's go and have some fun. I am way overdue." When they walked outside to the garage, the weather was nice so Jada decided to drive her Corvette with the top down. They didn't have to worry about their hair blowing because both had their hair in pinned up styles looking like they had just stepped out of the beauty shop. That is something that they picked up in college. Learning how to do quick styles kept them busy during their college days. The two best friends left driving to Club Stallion talking all the way about the first time they went to the club and how things had changed since then. Not only did Jada get that fine man but is about to become his wifey. What more is there to ask for?

Chapter 23

Des followed behind CJ. She dialed him on her cell. "CJ, you can go on home, I will come over later. I have a few stops to make."

"Des you don't know what I have planned for today. Oh, I forgot, I just bought you a brand new car. Alright", he hung up. He didn't like that at all. "Yeah that's just like her to get what she wants and take off to God knows where with whoever", CJ thought. Des didn't care how he felt. She had other important things on her mind. She drove to the church. She scanned the parking lot and there were only a few cars. She parked and noticed that the reserved for the pastor space was empty. She sat for a few minutes. Afterwards, she saw a grey Benz drive up with a handsome young man sitting behind the driver's seat. She put her head down like she was reading something. He waved to her probably thinking that she was one of his members. Rev had just that many members. No this couldn't be my brother. He stepped out in a gray tow piece silk leisure suit with some gator sandal style shoes headed inside the church. "This has to be my brother. My daddy must have been a fine man", she thought. "My brother sure is fine", she got out of her car and walked inside of the church to see what was going on. There were more people inside than she anticipated. She found her a seat in the back. He was teaching bible study. She caught the part where he talked about loving your enemies. She listened and couldn't take it anymore. She started crying, so she got up and walked out of the sanctuary to her car where she sat crying her eyes out. This was the first time she ever saw one of her brothers and it was more detrimental than she thought it would be. It was heartbreaking to know that he didn't know that he didn't know her. She thought about how her husband wanted to hurt her brothers and she doesn't even know them. She blamed them at first, but now after seeing him, she couldn't. Her granny would never have been proud of her for wanting them to pay for her being an outcast. Whatever happen between her mom and dad had nothing to do with her or her brothers. "I have got to stop him before something bad happens. This is my only family and they have a nephew that they do not know about. They will simply fall in love with him!" A deacon knocked on her window. "Sister are you ok?" She looked up at him with her red teary eyes. "Yes sir I am", she started her new car and drove away. She had one more stop to make.

Chapter 24

Jada and Chi Chi made it to the club. "Talking about reminding us of the first time we arrived. Nothing has changed. Look", Chi Chi pointed to Goldie. He stood in the same spot dressed in the expensive suit waiting to valet her car. Noticing who they were, "good evening ladies."

"Hello Goldie", Jada said.

"I guess congratulations would be in order for both occasions."

"Why thank you, Goldie", Jada replied. He looked at Chi Chi with a smile. "So how is Atlanta treating you?"

"Just fine, thank you"

"I can see that with that big rock on your finger. I heard that you tied the knot."

"Yes, I did." They got out and he got inside of the car and drove away. They walked inside of the club. "Let's sit downstairs and wait for Aaron", Jada suggested. After they found a seat, the phone behind the bar rang. The bartender could be overheard saying, "alright". After hanging up the phone, he walked to the edge of the bar. "Maliek said he will be down shortly."

"There he is watching you on that electronic monitor again." They both laughed. Chi Chi started popping her finger to the tune of R Kelly. "It's one thing about club

Stallion, they love R. Kelly. Girl, I don't know why you are looking at me like that, I am ready to get my party on", she said pointing at Jada's stomach who wasn't showing yet. "Stop it, Chi Chi." The bartender approached them. "What can I get for you ladies, this evening?"

"A virgin Strawberry Daiquiri for her and I will take a Long Island Iced Tea". Ten minutes passed and Aaron finally showed up with Regina. She had her nose stuck in the air. "Regina, you remember my sister Jada?"

"Yes, Hi Jada"

"And this is her best friend Chi Chi."

"Hello Cha Cha"

"Excuse me, my name is Chi Chi."

"Oh my bad", she replied sarcastically. She stood so close to Aaron, there was no room left between them. "Aaron can we go sit at a table?" She told him.

"Here are two seats".

"Aaron, I don't do bar stools". She started to walk off towards an empty table.

"Aaron, you need to check your chick before I do with her snobby acting self", Chi Chi said seriously.

"Chi don't worry about her". He ordered two drinks and took them to the table where she was sitting. Why did the DJ bust *The Stepper's Song* by R. Kelly? Two guys walked up to Jada and Chi Chi while they were dancing. They always thought they could step alone. "Girl you know this is our song". By the time the song was over, Maliek was standing at the bar. The look on his face was not a very happy one. He just didn't say anything. Chi Chi danced song after song like she was having the time of her life. She and Aaron started dancing and stayed on the floor. Regina got so heated that she decided to leave. She walked to the floor and told Aaron, "I will see you later. Call me when you get a chance. I will be at home." She rolled her eyes at Chi Chi. "Bye", Chi Chi said to her.

"What?" She said to Chi Chi.

"Regina just go if you are going." Aaron said to her. She saw the look that he gave her and walked off. It was fine with him that she was leaving. He was starting to enjoy partying with Chi Chi. After their last dance, they walked back to the bar where Jada was sitting and Maliek stood. "Aaron can you give Chi Chi a ride back to the mansion I see she is not ready to go?"

"Sure isn't, girl. I don't know the last time that I have danced like this."

"Yes Jada, I will make sure she gets back safely." He and Maliek shook hands. "My man", Maliek told him. "We will see you party animals later." The couple of the year walked out of the club hand in hand. "Jada I don't want you to over exert yourself. All of that dancing can tire you out."

"Maliek are you sure that is what you are concerned about?" He didn't answer her but she could tell by the look, he had a little jealous streak in him. Once they reached the outside, both of their cars were running and waiting.

Chapter 25

Desarie sat in her new caddy across the street from Club Stallion. After her last experience with CJ she was really saddened by seeing James. She did not know what exactly she was feeling right now but, right now, she did not want her husband messing with her brothers. She glanced across the street and she watched two gentlemen pull in the driveway, one in a red Corvette and the other in a red Ferrari that had Montana written on the license plate. She saw a beautiful young lady and a handsome young man holding hands while laughing, talking, and walking towards the Corvette. He fastened her seatbelt and kissed her on the lips then he walked back to the other car behind and got in. "Wow, this must be my other brother." She shed some more tears. She thought about her looks and she did favor the two men. She pulled out behind him and followed them out of the city to the mansion. She stopped at a far distance noticing that Montana Estates was engraved on the top of the electronic gates. For the first time in her entire life, she saw both of her brothers and felt a closeness to them. She longed to run up to both of them and tell them that she was their sister, but they probably wouldn't believe her without proof. She cried all the way while driving home so much, she had to pull over twice. She repeated to herself, "I do have family left. What am I going to do?" After pulling in her driveway, she sat and wiped her face with some Kleenex trying to get her composure before going in the house to get Juquan. He was the only one that could give her comfort now. She just wanted to lay down and hold her baby boy. When she walked into her house, she put him in her bed and checked both of her messages. She had all kinds of messages from CJ. She wasn't in the mood for his nonsense right now. She felt like she had just left a funeral. Drained, she held her son close while drifting off to sleep.

CJ had been drinking and pacing the floor since he made it back to his townhouse pissed off at Des.

"I buy her a new care and she run off. I guess she went to see her boyfriend. I should have known she was messing with someone. All the time I was gone, someone was hitting it. And she tell me I don't have no one, CJ. Yeah, right. I should just take my son and leave her here losing her mind."

He picked up his phone and dialed her house again then her cell phone. No answer.

"Forget this!"

He grabbed his keys and flew out of the door. He drove to Des' house and saw her car parked in the driveway.

"Now I can catch her with her panties down!" He left his car running and walked to the door. "Boom, Boom!" He banged the door extra hard. He didn't get a response fast enough, so he kicked her door and when she heard that, she jumped up. Then, he saw a light come on. She grabbed her robe and slipped into her bedroom slippers. She closed the door very lightly trying not to disturb Juquan. She walked to the door as fast as she could knowing that it could not be anyone else but CJ. She opened the door. He stepped in and started looking around. "What are you trying to pull, Des?" I have been trying to call you all evening and you did not have the decency to pick up the phone!"

"CJ, calm down and don't wake Juquan up. What is wrong with you coming all up in here like that? You are going to stop hollering in my house. I know you have been drinking that is why I left before and here you are again."

Des' phone rang and Des could see it was Nana. "No, Nana, everything is ok."

"No", she replied and she hung up.

"Des, where have you been", he asked her.

"CJ, this is not the time or the place. I told you, I had some stops to make. I don't have to answer to you. What you think cause you bought me a car and gave me some money you own me? You are losing your mind. Now you went and kidnapped my brother's girlfriend and on the run...."

"Hold up. I did that for you!"

"You are a lie. I never wanted you to do anything to hurt my family."

"Oh so, I see they are your family now. They don't know you. All of a sudden you are one of them?" He grabbed her by her robe.

"Let me go CJ and get out of my house!"

He pushed her and let her go. At the same time, he was sweating like a mad man. He walked out the door and looked and saw Nana standing on her porch with a shot gun. He had a flash back. He hurried to his car and as he was getting in, "I know you are not coming around her again. I will shoot you this time." CJ pulled off real fast not knowing where he was going. He was too angry to drive home. All he wanted now was a drink.

Nana walked over to Des' house carrying the same shot gun. Des finally broke down and told her the whole story. All Nana could say was "um, um, um, what chile?" They talked a long time before Des convinced her to go home and get some rest.

Chapter 26

Chi Chi and Aaron danced as if there was no tomorrow. But, the drinks had started kicking in. "Chi Chi are you ready to go? I think I have had enough and I have to drive."

"Yeah, I am getting a little tired", she said with her voice slurring. After they got in the car, she told him, "Aaron you really don't have to drive to the mansion right now." She was thinking about the long drive, plus, the condo was not that far. "You can take me back early in the morning. Remember, I used to live there."

"Ok well, if that is ok with you, it's fine with me." He said with relief. He headed toward the condo. Chi Chi adjusted her seat and laid back while he drove. He adjusted the radio to 92.3 FM and the slow jams were soothing. She moved her head to the beat until she didn't notice that the car was coming to a stop. "We're here", he said. Turning her head around looking. "I guess we are". They got out. He automatically locked the car. They walked to the door. He started fumbling with the keys. She went to look in her purse and realized that she never carried her keys to the condo anymore. She left them hanging in her kitchen in Atlanta. He finally found the right key to open the door. "I'm at home", she said dancing around like she had a burst of energy. He turned on the radio to the same station they were listening to in the car. The music was still on blast. "Yeah, Chi Chi you lived here for a few years so you know where everything is." Aaron walked to the kitchen and Chi Chi grabbed his hand and started stepping. "Come on Aaron". He pulled away. "I will be right back". He returned with two glasses filled with Cristal. "Here, we are going to have a night cap".

"Thank you", she said taking the glass out of his hand. She continued swaying her hips to the music. "Aaron sat and watched. "Do you feel like this all the time after going out on the town?" He asked her.

"No, I don't get to go out like this anymore. That is why I am enjoying this night." She took a sip spinning around. "Oh no they didn't."

"What are you talking about?" She sat her drink on the table. This is my song, *Love Won't Let Me Wait* by Luther Vandross. She grabbed his hand and pulled him off of the sectional sofa. She put her arms around his neck and he grabbed her around the waist. She sang along with the record, "We'll take a flight and spend the night in wonderland". She could feel the heat from his breath behind her ear. This dance was only the beginning of some serious love making. In this moment of passion, he started to unzip her dress. Closely she felt the rock that was brushing up against her thighs. She unzipped his pants and he stood straight out from his boxers. That really turned her on. She started to massage his penis with one hand and pulled his pants and boxers off with the other free hand. He got anxious and finished undressing himself. They dropped down on the real fur lion skin that Jada had in front of the fireplace. "I have been wanting this for a long time", he said while kissing her on her breast. "Yes, this is way overdue", she told him. She moaned as he started rubbing himself against her clitoris. After the wetness started flowing, he entered her. "Yes, Aaron I need it". He did her inch by inch. She raised her legs and wrapped them around his buttocks. He went in and out of her for a long time until they both hollered. There was no more energy left for dancing or drinking. They fell asleep for about four hours. She opened her eyes and captured what had taken place. She grabbed her clothes and ran into the bathroom and locked the door. Looking in the mirror, "what have I done?" "Oh my god, my husband!" She splashed water on her face but the water began to mix with the tears that flowed down her cheeks. She stepped in the shower feeling the guilt and shame reality kick in. She stepped out and dried herself off and got dressed. She opened the medicine cabinet and found some Visine and Tylenol. Once she felt she had it together, she walked back to where Aaron was still sleeping. "Aaron, Aaron wake up. I have to go. "He turned over and opened his eyes half way, "what's wrong?"

"Nothing, I just have to leave."

"Ok, Ok." He got up and grabbed his clothes going into the bathroom. "That was too much", he said to himself. Now she has that "It's your fault" look on her face. He washed up. "I can get in the shower when I come back. Boy am I drained." When he came out of the bathroom, she was standing at the door with her Coach bag on her shoulder. They walked to the car and the ride all the way to the mansion was in silence. He looked at her before she got out of the car. "You alright?" She didn't even answer. She nodded her head as to say yes but he knew better from her facial expression. She walked towards the mansion and never looked back when she entered. Everyone seemed to be sleeping. She tipped up the stairs and into the room from which she slept. She undressed and got in the bed balling up in a knot. She kept seeing her husband's face in a vision. She couldn't believe she had let herself go like this. Aaron pulled off shaking his head. Mrs. James heard the sound of the door. "Um, Um, Um, that boy of mine."

Chapter 27

Stan drove to several of his favorite hangout spots. Then he drove to a bar, he hadn't visited in quite some time. Matter of fact, it has been years since he even thought about entering TJ's and he wanted to respect Tracey's wishes to give her the evening alone with Ali. Once he left the bar, he would go crash at one of his girl's places. He sat at the bar on the far end watching the guy across the room shoot pool by himself. He thought about approaching him and challenging him to a game, but for now he was going to have himself a few drinks to get in the mood.

After CJ left Des's house with a serious attitude, he finally stopped at a bar to have one drink. But, CJ never had one drink. He stopped at TJ's parked and went into the bar. There was a seat on the far end of the bar where a young man was sitting having a drink. He had a seat with his face looking at the bartender. "How are you doing?" The man next to him asked.

"Well, I've had better days…women", CJ said.

"Yeah man, they could be a pistol sometimes."

The bartender came over and took his order after he drank his first swallow, he looked at the young man and said, "Man do you know, I just bought my wife a new car today, and she took off to who knows where and who know who she was with".

"Why am I telling you my problem? You probably have enough of your own. Most of us that sit in bars do."

"Naw man, I don't mind. My name is Stanley, most people call me Stan."

"Well, I'm Charles, Charles Knox". They shook hands. The two men started talking. They found out they use to hang out in the same parts of the city but they didn't know each other personally. CJ was careful of what he told him about himself. He had to be very careful knowing he was wanted by the police and it was too much money on his head. And when the Feds look for someone, they are thorough. They continued to talk and drink and the conversation got deep. "Man, I wish I could hit me another lick."

"Well, man I wouldn't call it a lick. Just say another little reward. You see there was these two guys that kidnapped a friend of my boss's girl. And one of the guys was at the Anaheim hotel spending mad cash on dancers, so my sister got turned on to him by another dancer and she set him up for the guys that was looking for them and that reward was very large."

"Is that right? I wish I knew where the guy was, I would have did the same thing", CJ said.

"Well the guy was real lucky. When they got to him, before anything could really jump off, the feds walked in while they was putting it down on him."

"You don't say", CJ replied raising his right brow.

"What happened to the other guy that was involved", CJ asked.

"Oh man, I don't know, but they are looking for him and that reward is also large." Stan had let the alcohol take over too much this time. He had talked a little too much. If only he knew he was talking to that other kidnapper, he would run to the phone to call Ali and collect his money. After this information, CJ offered to buy Stan double shots of liquor.

"Stan now tell me what is this man's name that girl got kidnapped?" CJ continued to question him.

"You know dude that owns Club Stallion downtown. I know you know. Everybody knows about Club Stallion. It's the hottest club in the 'D'."

"Yeah, I know. I haven't actually been to the club, but I heard a lot about it. Man, sound like you sister was smart. What is her name?"

"Her name is Tracey. She goes with Maliek's right hand man."

"You mean to tell me, he let her dance and get caught up in other people's situations like that?"

"To tell you the truth, at that time, he wasn't her man when all of this went down. They recently hooked up and they are already in love."

Stan didn't know, he was being used for information. The more he talked, the more information was being pumped out of him. CJ kept buying him drinks until,

Stan felt the alcohol take effect. "Well man, it was nice talking to you and I hope to see you sometime." Stan was felling drunk by now, so when he got up to walk out, he grabbed each chair for leverage as he walked to the exit. CJ was right behind him. "Man are you sure you can drive home?"

"Yeah, I'm alright. My car is right over here." He made it to his car and started fumbling with his keys. All of a sudden, he felt someone pop him on the head. It made a loud noise. CJ hit him again. Pop!!! Stan grabbed his head. Pop!!! He hit him again and this time Stan fell down beside the car. "Man, what are you doing?" Blood started spattering all over the Caprice Classic. The grey color turned into a bright red. "I tell you what I am doing. The guy you and your sister sold out was my partner." He kicked him in the face. A car light came on when he wiped his gun off on Stan's shirt and whispered in ear, "tell them CJ is back", then he ran to his car. "Somebody, get this man some help", a lady screamed. She watched the unidentified man run away and tried to get his license plate number but he sped off too fast. All she could see was the car was black and it happened so fast, plus it was too dark to see who it was. The ambulance arrived shortly there afterwards. The EMIs put Stan on the stretcher and rushed him to the nearest hospital. He was still breathing but one more blunt to his head and he would have been a goner.

Chapter 28

Hours earlier Ali drove all over town looking and putting out the word to people he know in the streets of Detroit. If CJ is anywhere to be found, he knew someone would take just as before. He drove to Tracey's apartment excited to see her. She opened the door wearing a black lace and spandex blouse with a matching skirt. Grabbing her new man around his neck, he picked her up as he walked inside. When he put here down, he looked around and was very impressed with the way she had her place set up. It showed him that she could decorate with class. She walked to the smoked dining room table and picked up a small box that she had placed there earlier. "This is for you, baby. Open it." She stood there smiling at him as he opened the gift. The smell of fragrance came through the wrapping paper. It was the men's cologne by Vera Wang. "How did you know, I like anything other than Cool Water?"

"I notice a lot of things. Remember that I am getting to know my new man." She rubbed him across his chest. He stood up. "Come here, you", he grabbed her and kissed her breathless. "Are you ready to eat?"

"Yes, I am", he replied. She walked to the kitchen. He followed her. "Something smells good", he said. She had two steaks broiling in the oven. "Honey, go wash up", she said pointing in the direction of the bathroom. She then went into the refrigerator and pulled out the salad she tossed earlier and two different salad dressings. She also had garlic toast and homemade mashed potatoes. "Baby, I didn't know you knew how to cook."

"It's more to me that just this", she said rubbing the side of her hourglass shape. They sat down to eat. Ali blessed the food and they dug in. After his first bite, "um, you can cook, girl!"

"Thank you." When they finished eating and put everything away, she led him to her bedroom. She put on some nice soft music by Alicia Keyes. She had her bedroom set up with a Canopy with sheer curtains. She adjusted the pillars so that he could sit up. The show was about to begin. Tracey started dancing as if she was in the VIP section at the club, taking off her blouse and skirt exposing the black stocking and garters she wore underneath. She dropped all the way to the crouch of his pants rolling on top of him. Her phone rang but she ignored it and kept doing what she was doing. The caller hung up. Whoever it was will call back was her thought. "Forget that phone". She began to take her man's shirt off still moving her body to the music. Tracey wanted her man and this was their first time. Ali wanted her just as bad. They were so heated that once his pants were unzipped, he stood in full attention which was noticeable from the boxers he wore. She wasn't surprised by the large size and thickness of him. But, it was a little more than she thought. She continued to grind on top of him until his manhood found her entrance. She moaned as he pulled her hips deeper on to him. He begin to look into her eyes as she tried to pull back the opposite way. "I'm not going to hurt you. Just relax." Tracey never had a man this size but she was experiencing that it hurt so good. Once he was in, much as she could take, he slowly massaged her on him. "You're mine now, Tracey. That is why I waited so long", he said giving her chills all through her body. "Are you mine, Tracey?" He whispered with every stroke. "Yes, Yes!" They both begin to get an organism that flowed like a river. "Ohhh!" She screamed "Ali!" He then flipped her over and gave more of it to her until he came to the point of no return. Afterwards, he fell over the side of her all worn out and exhausted. The phone rang again. "I think you better get that this time", he said. She eased over and pick up the phone. "Hello. Yes, this is Tracey". She began screaming. "Oh no!" She passed the phone to Ali. The nurse at the hospital told him about the accident with Stanley. "Ok, we will be there in a minute." He hung up. She left to go to the bathroom and shower. He joined her. They didn't have time for romance only enough time to clean up and get to the hospital. They got dressed within minutes. Ali and Tracey walked into the hospital through the emergency entrance. She walked to the reception desk. "Do you have a Stanley Jacobs?" The lady looked through her glasses. "Did you say Jacobs?"

"Yes, Ma'am", Tracey replied. The lady went through her computer. "Oh, I remember, they have transferred him to ICU. Go down this hall and take the elevator to the left to the fifth floor." They did as they were instructed going to the nurse's station. They were given the room number. "One at a time", the nurse said. "He is sedated." Tracey ran to the room, when she looked at her brother, she didn't even recognize him. He was all bandaged up with medication dripping from his IV. She started crying aloud. Ali heard her, so he came into the room and got her. "Come on baby." He led her to the family waiting room. "Sit here. I will be back." He walked back to the room. Stan was rolling his head from side to side. "Don't hit me man. Calm down."

"It's going to be ok. It's me, Ali. Stan who did this to you?"

"CJ, CJ CJ is back" then he nodded off.

Ali couldn't believe what he just heard. "Just hold on man, I am going to get the nurse." He walked to the nurse's station and told her he was trying to talk and seemed to be having a spasm in his head. They immediately went to attend to him. Ali walked back to the family waiting room where Tracey was sitting crying her eyes out. He removed her hand seeing her blood shot red eyes. "Baby there is nothing for you to worry your pretty face about. I will take care of this." The doctor walked in and asked if she was the sister to Stanley Jacobs. "Yes, my name is Tracey Jacobs. How is my brother doing, doc? I need your honest opinion."

"Well it's a little early to say. Right now he is stable. He took a hard beating on his head and I don't know what his prognosis will be. We are going to keep him sedated for the rest of the morning. He will be sleeping a lot so if you want to go home for a few hours that will be ok.

He really needs the rest. "She laid her head into Ali's chest running tears down his silk shirt. He grabbed her chin. "Let's go. He will be ok and when the police come to question him, I do not want to be around. The Feds are going to take this over. It was CJ, the guy that kidnapped Jada."

"Did he tell you that?"

"Yes, he did."

"Alright, we can go and I will drive my car back up here. You understand don't you baby? You know that is how they got CJ's partner Doug, from following me? Ali baby, you don't have to worry but tell me this, how did he get a hold of my brother?"

"I don't have any idea. Let's just let your brother recover so that I can find out what really happened. I am going to get that clown."

She walked back to the room where Stan was and kissed him on his forehead. "Stan, I will be back. Just hang in there. You are all that I have." She watched him for a few more minutes and walked out. Ali was waiting for her in the hallway. He drove her home and they cuddled for the remainder of the morning. Today will be another major hunt for CJ. All Ali could think about was how close this man was and he had to be stopped.

Chapter 29

Maliek and Jada arose to a wonderful breakfast that was prepared by Sung. He served it on the terrace. The morning weather was warm with a small breeze just enough to touch the leaves on the trees. Mrs. James came to join them. "Good morning, you two. How are you?"

"Fine, Ma", they replied. Sung rolled the gold cart that carried grits, cheese eggs, sausage, bacon and fresh fruits and orange juice.

"Looks like someone has been taking lessons", Jada said. Maliek noticing the foods, smiled at Mrs. James. So she spoke up before they could make any more comments. "Yes, I have been showing him a few things." Maliek was the first to finish. "Well, I have to get to the club. Some of the guys that are giving me a bachelor party will be coming by the club."

"What bachelor party?" Jada said in a jealous tone.

"They think I should have a party being this is my first time getting married. What is wrong with that, baby? Now Jada come on."

"No Maliek, I guess nothing is wrong with that." He kissed her.

"I will see you later", stepping over to Mrs. James. He kissed her on the cheek. "Talk to your daughter."

"I will. Don't worry about her", she said to him before he left for work.

"Jada I know you are not getting mad at him because of a little party?"

"Mama, knowing Maliek and his friends, I doubt that there will be anything little about this party."

"Well, Jada never try to smother your man. The more freedom you let him have the better the relationship will be. How many times do I have to tell you that? Why don't you seem to believe me?"

"Oh, Ma. I believe you. Where is Chi Chi?" Jada said looking back into the glass door.

"Chile that girl didn't get in until the wee hours of the morning."

"How did you know that Ma?"

"Just how many times, I have to tell you Mama knows everything." After they finished talking and eating, "let me go check on Chi Chi". Jada went to the room where she slept and knocked lightly she didn't get an answer so she cracked the door open just enough to see her sleeping. She did not want to disturb her so she went into her bedroom to take her shower. As she walked out and started to get dressed, Chi Chi knocked. "Come in". She stepped in.

"Well the dead has risen. What is wrong with you? Look like you had a long night."

"Yeah, girl. I am officially hung over."

"What time did you get in?"

"I really don't know."

"I can tell. Your eyes are blood shot red."

"Yeah, I know", Chi Chi replied with a lazy look. Jada noticed that she wasn't her usual cheerful self.

"So I take it that Aaron saw you home ok?"

"What?" Sounding harshly at the mention of his name.

"Chi Chi what is wrong?"

"I'm ok and yeah, he saw me home ok. I'm sorry Jada if I sound harsh. It's just I am still really tired from all that partying."

"Go get yourself together and I am going to take you and Mama shopping so we can pick out her dress for the wedding. I am also going to call Deb to have our hair and nails done. In case you did not notice, young lady, I haven't taken you shopping since you have been here and you have organized your behind off for me. I want you to know that I really appreciate everything that you are doing."

"Jada, what are friends for? Give me about one hour and I will have myself together." Chi Chi left.

Jada hit the intercom button to her mother's room. "Mama get ready. We are going out shopping today to get your dress and have our hair done."

"Girl, don't worry about me, I will be ready before you hit the steps", her mother said excited. Once they all got dressed, Jada tried to decide which vehicle to take because she knew how she and Chi Chi shops. There will be a lot of packages so she decided to drive Maliek's grey Escalade. It hasn't been driven much since the delivery. It would have plenty of room for the bags. They drove to Monique's Hair Salon first. Deborah put the whip on their hair, one at a time. Mrs. James looked twenty years younger with her new style. "Mama, you look so good!" She patted the sides of hair. "Baby, I know!" Chi Chi still was not her cheerful self and Jada knew it. She had been around her friend long enough to know when something is bothering her. Whatever it was she sure wasn't ready to talk about it even though Jada had made plenty of hints. Jada then drove to Troy, MI to Big Beaver Road to Somerset Mall. If her Mom was going to wear a dress it had to come from Saks Fifth Avenue. They were approached by a clerk. Jada explained to her what the colors of her wedding would be, she nodded her head and told them that she would be right back. When she returned, she had a whole outfit that would be perfect for the occasion. The dress was a shaded purple sequence with a hat to match. They followed her to the dressing room. "Ma, try it on. That dress is beautiful."

"Sure is", Chi Chi said. Mrs. James walked into the dressing room and when she came out, she looked very elegant. It also made her shape stand out tremendously well.

"That's it", they said in unison. She modeled back and forth. When she did her last spin, "Mama, that's enough." "You are going to wear yourself out before you can get the dress off." She put her hands on her hip. "No, not Ms. Clara James." The clerk found humor in her customers. Once Mrs. James passed her the dress back, she looked at tag twice thinking maybe this was too much. Jada quickly burst her bubble when she said "we will take it and we need shoes to match." The total bill came to thirty eight hundred dollars. But it didn't matter. Anything for her mother. You only get one. "What a lovely daughter you have. I can't remember my daughter treating me ever to some grands in shopping sprees and it's not like she couldn't afford to. She spends it all on herself."

"I am sorry to hear that, Ma'am. I hope that God change her heart", Mrs. James replied. She passed Jada the garment bag and a shopping bag. "You ladies have a good day and thank you for shopping at Saks Fifth Avenue."

"Thank you too", Jada told her. Mrs. James grabbed the shopping bag out of Jada's hand and winked at the clerk. Now it was shopping time. They had gotten Mama out of the way. Jada and Chi Chi started their spree. They bought all kinds of clothes that they didn't need. Jada's excuse was she need larger clothes for the weight she was about to gain and Chi Chi didn't have an excuse. She just loved to shop and after the fifth store, she brightened up a little. Maybe the shopping relieved some of the tension and stress she was carrying around. They had lunch at Red Lobster. "Girl that baby is going to come out looking like a lobster", her mother said. "I don't care, just as long as it's a healthy and normal baby." On the way home, Jada mentioned stopping by the condo to see Aaron. Chi Chi spoke up fast. "I'm a little tired and I have to get packed for my trip home." The tone she said it raised a flag in Jada's head. She knew her friend. Something was wrong and she would eventually find out. The two of them never kept secrets long. Jada didn't comment. She started driving towards the mansion. Mom broke the silence. "Girl do yall ever listen to Steve Harvey on the radio in the morning? I really enjoy listening to him and Tommy."

"Mama, I think he comes on at 6:30am. I use to listen to them all the time while I got dressed for work", Jada said.

"Well I don't miss a morning. I might even send a strawberry letter." Both of the girls started laughing. "What yall laughing at. I'm serious."

"Ma, what kind of letter you're going to send to the show. It better be right because Steve will put a lid on it."

"Make sure you call me in Atlanta when she does send one. I don't want to miss out on that", Chi Chi said. As they drove up in front of the mansion, Sung came out to help them carry the packages. He took Mrs. James' first. Jada looked at her mother and said, "If you keep this up, I will be sending a Strawberry letter on you." Mrs. James shook her head walking in front of them. After everything was in, Mrs. James went to take a nap. Jada told Chi Chi to meet her in the den. She wanted to talk to her. Once they met and was seated, "Girl did something happen between you and my brother last night?"

"Why would you ask me something like that?"

"Because you showed it all with the mention of his name and when I asked you all about stopping by my condo I knew something right then. If something happened, then girl we need to talk about it. I know when something is wrong with you and you know it, so spit it out."

"Well, Jada I don't know how to begin to tell you this." She broke down and started crying. Jada moved over to the part of the sectional where she sat and hugged her. "What happened, girl?"

"I don't know and I can't lay it on the drinking I knew quite well what I was doing. I guess I have not been getting enough from my husband. I was in heat but that is not an excuse. I married him to be a faithful wife."

"Chi Chi did you use protection?"

"No, we didn't. It happened so fast, I couldn't help myself."

"What if you get pregnant by my brother? You told me, you stopped taking your pills."

"I don't know Jada. I feel awful and the guilt is eating me up. I am a married woman and gave myself to another man and it wasn't a quickie. I feel so bad, I just want to go home tonight."

"Well if you feel like it will make you feel better then you can leave tonight. The wedding is only two weeks away and one more night won't change anything here."

"You have done just about everything you could. Are you upset with me Jada?"

"No, Chi Chi. I don't like what happened but you put yourself in that position and part of it is my fault. I should have left you my car."

"No Jada do not start blaming yourself. I did it and I have to deal with it and now I have to face my husband."

"Girl, you act like he caught you or something."

"I guess you have a point but I know one thing for sure. I have to stay away from your brother. His sex is addictive."

"Just make sure it don't happen again", Jada said to her. The two friends went upstairs so that Chi Chi could pack and call the airlines. She dialed Delta. "I can leave tonight at 7:00pm", telling Jada holding the phone after she confirmed the flight and hung up. "I will drive you to the airport."

"No you won't, I can use your driver. You have done enough running today."

"Alright if you insist. Pass me the phone, I will call him right now." She passed Jada the phone. She dialed their personal driver after hanging up. "He will be here at 5:30pm." Jada looked at her and joked, "do you want Aaron to drive you to the airport?"

"Yeah right". They both laughed. Chi Chi was relieved and feeling better that she had talked about what happened. They spent the rest of the evening tying up the loose ends of the wedding. "I will be back the Wednesday before the wedding."

"Ok that will be fine. I will miss you as usual, Jada told her giving her a hug. The hours went by fast but everything related to the planning was taken care of by the time, the Limo arrived, on time as usual. Jada and Mrs. James walked her to the car. "Thank you so much girl. I couldn't have did this without you." They all hugged. All of them hated good-byes. Aaron drove up just as Chi Chi was getting in the car. "Where are you going", he asked.

"Home to my husband", she said with a smile. The driver closed the door.

"I thought she was staying a couple more days", he said.

"No she got to get back to her husband, Aaron", Jada said in a smart way. He looked at her like "where did that come from!"

Chapter 30

Ali woke up after trying to get a couple of hours of sleep. He glanced at Tracey and thought to himself, she is one fine specimen. At the moment, he tried to ease out of the bed, it alarmed her. "Just where do you think you are going? When you move I move." He then turned and kissed her. "Good morning, sweetheart. Did you get a little rest", he asked.

"Yes, I nodded a few times and so did you." Her mind wondered to her brother. "Oh my God, I have to get to the hospital!" Both of them got up, got into the shower and go dressed. "Let me take you to IHOP to get something to eat before you go to the hospital."

"Ok, that sounds good."

They drove separate cars headed to IHOP for breakfast. After they were seated and ordered, Ali said, "Baby when you get to the hospital, call me and keep me posted and let me know how Stan is doing. I am going to be real busy trying to catch up to this monster that did this to him along with all of the other dirt he has done. He really thinks he can get away with all of this." She tilted her head to the side, "baby just be careful. I am not ready to lose you."

"Tracey trust me, I have been a bodyguard for many of years and I can very well handle myself and other people's situations and I am for sure going to take care of you too." She grabbed his face and kissed him across the table. The waitress stood there and watched, "excuse me, can I get you something else?" They kept kissing then finally stopped and said "no thanks." She could see love at its newest point. When they finished, Ali paid for the meal and they left going separate ways. When Ali reached the club, Maliek was already in his office. He knocked on the door, "man, you are not going to believe what happened last night."

"What?"

"My girl Tracey's Brother Stan, you remember him?"

"The one that hooked me up with the information, yes", he said.

"Well last night Stan met CJ at a bar not planned. I don't know how CJ knew who he was but apparently CJ must have waited on him outside the bar. He beat him half to death with a pistol. I was with his sister at the time and the hospital called. When I got to the hospital, Stan was woke. He told me CJ was the one who attacked him!"

"How did this happen?" Maliek started pacing the floor stopping in front of his desk. He hit the desk with his fist. "I don't believe this slime still would even have the nerve to come back to Detroit and just act like he is untouchable! Man, I want him real bad. I wouldn't be surprised if he would have been all up in my club."

"I just thought I would tell you the news. I am going back out to hit the streets and see if anyone has anymore information on him."

"Ali, you must not be offering enough money out there. I told you I don't care how much it costs. Find that trick. Where is Goldie?"

"Oh, I think he was driving up when I was coming in."

"Take him out with you today. Two heads are better than one."

"Alright man, I will call and keep you posted", Ali said.

"Man, what is Stan's last name", Maliek questioned. "His name is Stanley Jacobs."

"I want to call and make sure his hospital bills are paid and I hope he will be ok."

"Did he say how the man looked?"

"No, he only told me who it was and he drifted back out."

"Alright man, I'm out. He gave Maliek a dap and left. Once he reached the downstairs, he saw Goldie. He filled him in on what happened. They left on their mission. Maliek called the hospital and notified them to send the bill to him. He also wanted Stan to have the best doctors and treatment. Being a man with money, he knew they would treat him differently.

Chapter 31

Ali called Tracey to check on Stan's condition and to see if he was awake.

"Yes, he is, thank God, Baby. And, I know the name of the bar where it happened." He pulled out his pad and wrote down the information. When he and Goldie arrived at TJ's, there was a closed sign on the door but they peeked through the door and noticed that there was a man inside. Once Goldie hit the door, the man came to the door. "We are not open yet. Come back in one hour and we will be open for business." They pushed their way in. "What do you guns want", the middle aged man scorned.

"Are you cleaning up or did you work here last night", Ali asked him.

"Both, I work and clean up here, why?"

"We want to know about the two guns that were here last night. One of the men was hurt real bad", Ali said.

"I don't know nothing and you have to leave", the man answered. Ali grabbed him by his collar. "Either you tell us what we want to hear or you are going to have some problems."

"Alright, Alright! One minute, I think one of them dropped something." Ali let his collar go and he walked behind the bar and got a wallet which had little money inside. There was just a few twenty dollar bills inside and a card for the office of Bloomfield Townhouses, no ID or anything else. The card was a start. One thing they knew was Stan didn't stay in Bloomfield Townhouses. This wallet had to belong to CJ. "They say the man was driving a black car", the man said.

"Yeah thanks for the information", Ali said reaching in his pocket and passing the man one hundred dollars. The man got excited at the bill. "Man is there anything else I can do? My name is Leo." The two men nodded their heads and left the bar. After Ali and Goldie got inside of the car, "man I think we just got lucky. That has to be that trick's hid out."

"Bet that", Goldie replied. They drove to Bloomfield Townhouses. While Ali drove through, he told Goldie, "man look for a black car." They went through every entrance. When they reached the last entrance there was a bald head man pulling out in a Chrysler 300LS. They didn't recognize his face, but it had to be CJ. CJ spotted them first and began to drive fast. That was their clue that it was him. Goldie shot his back window out. Glass splattered everywhere. Boom! Boom! Boom! There were shots going everywhere all through his new car. CJ drove as fast as he could saying to himself, "just let me make it to the expressway then I can shoot back or lose them!"

"If you want to catch him, you got to drive a little faster Goldie". "Man don't worry about shooting." Both of them had their guns out shooting but as they came to the light it changed from yellow to red. Ali knew he couldn't run the light in this part of town plus a police cruiser was headed towards the townhouses. Someone must have called about the shooting. CJ was lucky he was in time for the light. Ali hit the steering wheel. "That was him! We almost had him."

"Guess what? We know where he lives." They gave each other high fives and got on the expressway.

CJ's heart was racing real fast as he drove his shot up car. He drove as fast as the speed limit would allow him to go. "How in the hell did they find out where I live? What am I going to do?" Then someone came to mind. "Oh I know someone." He drove to the eastside to an old man that he use to know. Mr. T used fix on cars and if he was still living. He knew he had a couple of garages and rooming houses. He drove through the alley. He could see old man Tripplet was still in business. He parked behind the garage. Mr. T. got up from where he was sitting. "Who you", not recognizing CJ was. "Mr. Tripplet you remember the bar on the west side you used to come to every evening? Remember the bartender named CJ? Well, this is me, CJ." Mr. T glanced through his glasses. "You don't look the same."

"I know. Do you remember Betty Jean, the neighborhood girl, I introduced you to?"

"Yeah, yeah I remember now. Big butt Betty Jean. Um, um, um, that girl had some butt on her. Man, what's up?" He shook CJ's hand. Finally, now that Mr. T. remembered CJ's mind was a little at ease. He looked at CJ's car. "Man what happened to that nice car you driving?"

"Well, Mr. T., I loaned it out and the guy that was driving got involved in a shootout."

"Did he get shot? I know he did from all of those bullet holes."

"Yes, he did. I am lucky to have my car back", CJ lying with a grin on his face. "Mr. T., I need a favor from you. I need to put my car in your shop and see if you have one to loan me."

"Well, I don't know CJ", he replied. CJ pulled out a knot of money.

"I reckon I can come up with something", he said after seeing all of the money in CJ's hand. "Pull in the garage next to the corner. I own all of these houses now. You wouldn't be looking for a room or something?" Mr. T. was a very wise man. He could pick up on when someone was in trouble. He also remembered how CJ used to treat him some nights when he got drunk. He would drive him home and catch a cab back. More than that, he really remembers the girls he used to get for him.

"Mr. T., I am looking for a place for a couple of weeks until I get ready to leave town."

"Oh, you are leaving the big city", he asked.

"Yes, I am. I have had enough of the D for a while." CJ noticed how time had changed Mr. T. He had turned all the way gray and seemed not to be the same spunky man he used to know. He now walked with a cane. But one thing was the same, he was still active working on cars and most surely still tricking with young women. "Let's walk down here and see if I can find you a get around car." He opened the garage two doors down and there were two old classics sitting there. One was a nineteen eighty Buick Regal and a nineteen seventy Skylark. "You can drive that Regal for awhile until I can repair your car. But you know it's gonna cost you cause I know you are still getting your hustle on day by day and when you get old like me, you just sit back and collect all you can. We always have something a younger man can use and that is knowledge to give away."

"Mr. T., since you are so nice, here is two grand for my car repairs and you can let me know when you need some more and here is a grand for the room." He rubbed the money together. "Now that's what I am talking about", counting the money after he put it in his wallet. "Now let's go to see the room I have for you. It will be like your own apartment. No one lives up there. "They walked into the house in front of the garage and went upstairs. Mr. T. sure had good taste. The whole place was carpeted in blue and there were two bedrooms and a kitchen and bathroom which would be shared with another tenant if one moves in, a small dining room area with a glass table for two that sits about five feet high. He opened the door to the room and it was furnished with a black Lacquer bedroom set. "This bedroom set was bought for one of the young girls

I used to screw but I found out she was sneaking a young man in the bed every chance she got and I moved this right back out. It cost me a pretty penny. It was only for me and her. You should have saw her standing in the doorway when my guys was moving the set out. She was half dressed and look like she had just got out of bed with someone. I caught her early in the morning. He probably was in the closet like the song. She kept saying come on T don't listen to people. They are lying. How am I going to pay my own rent? I told her get it how you live and walked out. That girl still calls me everyday begging me but little did she know, I saw her letting him out one morning and she didn't see me. They started laughing. What kind of fool did she think I was? He couldn't buy her a bed but was still getting the goodies. No way and the thing about it was she didn't have to see me but once a month and that was enough. I am an old man. I can't do much even with the Viagra." CJ stood there listening like he will be glad when this man stops talking. But another part of him knew if it wasn't for this talking old man, he would not have any place to go. Treating this old man nice in the bar has paid off. It is a true saying that you have to be careful how you treat people. CJ also thought about when he was on track and his life was going well. He used to be well loved. He was a good bartender, now he was out of control ever since he was fired from Club Stallion.

Chapter 32

CJ stood in the middle of the room after Mr. T. left thinking about how difficult this type of life was…being on the run and it wasn't very pleasant. He dialed Des and told her he needed to see her and wasn't at the townhouse. "I'll call you right back." She said Juquan was standing in front of her and looking in her mouth just as she hung up. "Was that my daddy on the phone?" Before she could answer the question, he said, "I dreamed that you and my daddy was arguing last night. It was really bad, Ma." She hugged him tight knowing that it wasn't a dream that it was true. "That's all it was baby a bad dream. Don't feel bad when Mama was little she used to have bad dreams."

"For real, Ma and you woke up crying?"

"Yeah for real", she answered rubbing his wavy hair. "Now I have to get you ready to go to Nana's house so I can take care some business."

"Ma, can I take care some business with you?"

"No, maybe I will take you somewhere later. I am not going to promise you but we will see what happens." She got him dressed and took him next door. She walked back to her house and phoned CJ. He picked up on the first ring. He gave her the address. She then drove to where he was. She parked in front and blew her car horn. Once he peered out of the window and saw who it was, he went outside and got in the car with her. "CJ what are you doing here?"

"Some of Maliek's guns found out that I live in the townhouses and I was leaving. They shot my car up and I got away just by an inch of time." She glanced him up and down to see if he was hurt.

"Are you alright", she asked.

"Yeah, I am alright but I don't know how long I can take this running from place to place. We have to go to the townhouse and get the rest of my money. "CJ I don't know if I am going to take that kind of chance."

"Des you have to. I can't even survive out here without money. Please Des, please. If you don't do anything, help me out. I doubt if they are back out there. Plus they didn't see which apartment I came out of. You can park on the other side and walk to the house."

"I guess I will try it but CJ I am not putting myself in any danger. I have a little boy that needs me alive. You should have thought about the consequence when you kidnapped that man's girl."

"Des, I am warning you. Don't start on me about that if you supposed to be my wife then you will do whatever it takes. You haven't turned any of my money down have you?"

"No CJ that is where you are wrong. You know I haven't been your wife for a long time." He raised his hand to hit her. "Do it CJ. Go right ahead and your day will be over today." He thought about it and knew he didn't have anyone else in his corner. "You know what Des, I can see you have gotten what you want from me and you cannot tell me you don't have another man."

"There you are accusing me again. Just the same old thing. This is why we can't be together."

"What did you say? Is that what you think? Don't make me do something to you that I will regret. You are not just going to ditch me and take my son away from me again." Des just continued to drive to the townhouse. She knew he had gone overboard. He was talking out of his head and it was scaring her. She needed to get rid of him and fast. She drove to the front entrance and around the opposite way from the normal. She would go in. CJ was ducked down. He would duck his head around looking paranoid and scary. "Park right here", he said in a loud tone.

"Look CJ, if you want my help, you're going to calm down and stop hollering at me and I mean just that." "You go ahead and walk through and open the door and I am right behind you." She got out and walked very calmly so no one would notice if they were watching. The same thing couldn't be said for CJ. He was ducking and looking through the peek hole. He ran upstairs and grabbed the few clothes he had and his money bag and laptop. He hollered downstairs, "go get the car. Don't just stand there!" She walked out saying under her breath, "I should leave him right here. I have had enough of his attitude." When she drove up in front, he was running out like he was running for his life. "Let's go!" She drove off in the Black Caddy unharmed. "Stop at the liquor store", he said. She didn't cross words with him but only catered to his request. He went in and came out with his usual, Jack Daniels. Once they reached the apartment, "are you coming in?"

"No, CJ. I have to get Juquan."

"Since when did you have to rush back to get him? Nana takes good care of him. What you want some money, Des? Matter of fact, take this money home with you." He took out some grands and gave her the bag. "Can I see you later", he asked.

"I don't know, CJ". He looked at her and got out and slammed her car door. She drove off fast trying to get away from him!

Chapter 33

Tracey arrived at the hospital. She stopped downstairs to get her only brother in the world a card and some balloons. She hurried upstairs and went into his room. He was sitting up in the chair. She was upset about it so she walked back to the nurse's station and asked "Why is Stanley Jacobs up? Is he strong enough and he is in a nod?" The head nurse was sitting looking in a chart. She looked on the board to see who was in charge of him and she paged the appropriate person. Once the nurse reached the station, "this is Stanly Jacob's sister. She would like to know why he is sitting up."

"The reason we sat him up is that the injury to the head was very damaging to his nervous system and sitting up will help him to start to repair the damage done to his system. We will be putting him down shortly. Right now he is slowly recovering."

"Ok, thank you. I will trust your judgement."

"One more thing Ms. Jacobs there is a gentleman paying all of your brother's expenses. His name is Maliek Montana."

"Oh really."

"Yes, he has called and made arrangements with our financial department. So we have called in another specialist."

"Thank you, nurse. That is good to hear." She walked back to the room and pulled up a chair beside him. She gave him a kiss on his forehead. "How's my favorite brother doing?"

"I'm here thank God for that", he said in a weak tone. "The police have been here to take my statement and asking all sorts of questions about that man but I don't know that much about him."

"Did they upset you or something?"

"No, not really. I just did not feel like all of that right now."

"Yeah, I know Horn. I wish I would have been here. I wouldn't have allowed them to bother you until you are feeling better. I was just told Maliek is sponsoring your bill. I met him and his girl. They are really cool people. Ali took me to their mansion for dinner."

"What, he did", Stan said.

"You go girl, in the big league."

"Let me tell you Stan, that place was out of sight. You should have been there. It had a swimming pool, sauna, tennis court, basketball court, mini football field and a couple of guest houses in the back. The main house had nine bedrooms and five of them had Jacuzzi tubs, a theater, two dens, one family room, study and check this out, the place was black and white marble all the way through. "

"I just can't imagine. Ali must be really in love with you to take you to his boss's house.

Chapter 34

Des drove around for awhile after dropping CJ off. She felt so distraught that she didn't know which way to go or who to turn to. Her nerves had not been this bad since she first left CJ. "I can see now that he has gone into one of his crazy modes. Something has to be done about him", she thought. She had noticed the dried blood on the gun when he pulled it out of the townhouse. "If I would have said something, he would have flipped out or started to lie which he is good at. What have I gotten myself into? I know one thing, he better not even have any thoughts about hurting either of my brothers. I just can't let that happen." The past has to stay the past. She drove pass her brother's church, circled the block and came back around. She saw two vehicles parked and a Navigator parked in the Pastor's reserved parking space. She sat there for a few minutes saying "I just got to talk to someone." She got out without her purse. She automatically locked the Caddy and walked to the side entrance. She went through the door looking around to find out where his office was located. Before she could see the office, a tall handsome man approached. She then realized, it was Rev Turner III. "Can I help you Miss?" Her tongue got stuck, "um….I was wondering if you do any kind of counseling?"

"Yes, I most certainly do."

"Do I need an appointment?"

"No since you are already here. Step into my office." He pointed to the door that she did not notice on the right side. She stepped inside and really admired his taste. His office was very exquisite and spacious. She admired the beautiful plants that hung all around the room. "How lovely."

"My name is James Turner III. I am the Senior Pastor here at Liberty Temple. May I ask whom you might be?"

"My name is Desarie", she hesitated, "Desarie Turner". He shook her hand. "Pleased to meet you", he said extending his hand towards her.

"You too, Rev Turner."

"Have a seat." She sat on the brown plush leather chair directly across from the Red Oak work desk.

"Thank you", she replied.

"Now tell me, what can I do for you?"

"I need to ask you the true meaning of forgiveness."

"To tell you the truth, my meaning for forgiveness is to give up all resentment you have toward anyone and Jesus said in the bible if you can't forgive your brothers and sister, he can't forgive you."

"Oh, I see", she said. "Well how about if you know someone that wants to hurt someone because of their past and that person don't have anything to do with why that person is resented?"

"Ms. Turner, is it ok if I call you Desarie?"

"Yes, that is fine."

"From my point, that is a part of forgiving. Let's just say why hold a grudge on something or someone that you can't change? And, I am a firm believer is the only thing you can do is forgive and try to do better. Even me as being a preacher, I have been in situations that seemed unforgiveable. But once I changed my life, it was easy to forgive. And, when we do, there is a peace and joy that is indescribable that comes over our being. Desarie, if you truly want to be blessed, you have ask God to give you a forgiving spirit." After he spoke those words to her, she had tears in her eyes. He passed her some Kleenex. "Is there anything else that you would like to discuss?" She wanted so hard to say "I am your sister", but she held back. "I hope that I was able to help you and feel free to come by any time. Here is a schedule of all of the services." He passed her a card. "Thank you, Rev. This has helped me." She stood up to leave. They took another long look at each other. She rushed out of the door. He was about to ask her some questions about which Turners she was related to but it was too late. In his mind, she reminded him of someone, he just couldn't put his finger on it. Des sat in her Caddy for a few minutes. She said a little prayer, "Lord show me the way to come into my two brothers' life."

Chapter 35

Ali and Goldie made it back to the club shortly after the little shooting incident with CJ. Maliek was sitting in his office doing payroll for the week. Ali called him to ask if he could come up. "Yes, you can if you hurry. I am going home early", he said. Ali entered his office and stood over his desk and told him what happened. "Man, I knew you find him. He is the slip up type, very careless."

"Yeah man, we just didn't see which apartment he came out of. But, I am sure of his new appearance. He has shaven his head and I think he had on a mustache. I couldn't really tell what other changes he has made. But believe me man, I know for sure he is back in Detroit."

"Ali, I don't want anything to happen on or before my wedding. Post someone there around the clock. Knowing CJ, he is running scared and probably not going back there any time soon. You just have to keep on looking until you find him. We don't want any surprises."

"Maliek I came this close to getting him today. I guess he bought a new car with the money, he got from you."

"Let him enjoy it while he can", Maliek said pushing away his desk. "I am going to get out of here. I haven't spent any time with Jada since Chi Chi was here helping her to plan the wedding. I think I am going to surprise her this evening. Here is all of the checks signed and sealed so you can take them to your office." He passed Ali the checks, "and remember, we are going to play ball tomorrow with my brother. Make it around three o'clock and bring your girl."

"Alright man, they left out of the office and went their separate ways."

Chapter 36

Everyone at the mansion was surprised to see Maliek back so soon. He walked inside. Jada saw him. "Hi baby", he said. She grabbed him around his neck. They kissed breathlessly. "Maliek are you alright?" He grabbed her again and kissed her. "Can a man come home early to spend some time with his babies?" He put a smile on her face that made her glow even more. "I want you to get dressed. I am going to take my favorite girl out." As they started up the staircase, the gate rang. Maliek answered the intercom, "yes may I help you?"

"I am Sergeant Long form the Sheriff's department and I have a subpoena to deliver to Ms. James." Maliek hit the enter button. "Come on up." He and Jada met the police at the door. "Ms. James, we have made several attempts to deliver you this subpoena to testify against Douglas Brenner. We had to go through Chase Bank because no one ever answered at the address we had at Harbor Town Condos. Just sign here." She signed on the line. "Thank you, Ma'am. Have a good day." The police got in his car and drove off. Maliek looked at the expression on Jada's face and rubbed her shoulders. All of a sudden, she felt pain. She probably had a flash back of her kidnapping and the thought of facing one of the men again was terrifying. Aaron and Mrs. James walked her to the closest den to sit her down. "Baby are you alright", he asked.

"Yes, I am. This has just come as a shock to me. I guess I never thought I would see that man again."

"Just relax sweetheart." Aaron walked back in, "here you go, sis." Maliek took the glass and held the cup up to her mouth. He sat down beside her and read the summons. It was set for Monday at nine o'clock. "If you don't feel like going out, we can do it another time."

"Just give me a little time and I will let you know if I feel like going out."

"Jada, we can always stay here. There is plenty to do here." She grabbed his hand, "baby I know you want to take me somewhere and I don't think I want to pass that up. It's not often we get to do something together. After debating they decided to have a nice quiet evening at home. "Maybe you will feel better tomorrow and we can go out."

"Ok I am so sorry that I spoiled your plans for me. Would you like me to make it up to you?"

"You have made it up to me", he said rubbing her stomach. Mrs. James and Aaron watched them play kissey, kissey. They had a certain look on their faces telling Jada that something was on their minds.

"What's wrong Ma?" Aaron spoke first.

"We have been trying to figure out how to tell you, we want to go home to check on the house for a few days."

"Why do you all feel like it is hard for me to understand? It's only for a couple of days. We don't mind, do we boo", she said to Maliek

"Yes that is ok and matter of fact, you don't have to fly this time. You can drive the same Benz, you have been driving." Jada said, "are you sure?" "Yes I am sure. When have you ever known me to act funny about anything materialistic?" He kissed her. "You are the one that's important to me and your happiness."

"When will you all be leaving, Aaron because you have to hurry and bring my mother back?"

"I knew with us being here this long, she would get attached. Don't worry, we will be back in plenty enough time for the wedding," Mrs. James said. "Aaron go and get the bags." Jada's eyes got large. "Ma, when were you going to tell me?"

"Actually I wasn't. I was going to leave you a note. Just kidding."

"Ok Mama, just hurry back."

"Yeah Ma, hurry back", he repeated. Aaron came back with their bags. "We are all set to go."

Maliek told them, he will be right back. He returned with an envelope. "Here this should help you on the way home." Aaron opened the envelope and saw the contents. He then passed it to his Mom. She looked at it, "Maliek what are you up to now!"

"It's only twenty five hundred little measly dollars."

"Where do you think we are going to L.A.?" Benton Harbor is only three hours away. "Well that is Ok. You never know what might happen on the road." She hugged him. "Jada is so lucky to have you and so am I."

"Yes Ma'am, we are all family now." Jada and Maliek walked them to the car. Jada was looking sad. Her mom kissed her. "Baby, I will be back before you miss me."

"I already do." They both stood and waved them goodbye. Maliek had his hand around Jada's waist. "Cheer up. It's okay for a week. We are getting married the following week."

"I guess you are right. I didn't realized it was right around the corner." Maliek kissed Jada all the way back inside while she backed up "how about us taking a swim and get in the hot tub. We have the whole mansion to ourselves." They walked to their pool area and changed into swimwear. They got the floats that lay back and put them in the pool. Maliek started sipping on some imported wine. Jada knew when he took the first drink it wouldn't be long before his nature would rise to its full capacity so she made the first move. She walked to the edge of the pool. He wasn't paying attention at the time, she slipped out of the two piece she wore and dropped them in the water so he would notice them floating. He jumped at the sight of the floating top and spilled his drink in the water. He looked up to the side of the pool and her beautiful fine frame showing all of her nakedness. She walked towards the bubbling hot tub without a word, she beckoned him with her finger as she took the stops going down. He jumped out of the pool and followed her. When he got to the steps, he undressed from the silk shorts he was wearing. "You are full of surprises."

"I have learned from the best", she said. Maliek cornered her in one corner of the tub and began kissing her all around her neck. She grabbed the side of his face and started kissing him on his face and on his head. Once she hit behind his neck, he was in full attention and ready to explore the inside of his woman. Maliek braced his hairy muscular legs and lifted her up to rest only on him. She grabbed him around his neck. He entered her with great passion. He began lifting her up and down slowly whispering in her ears. "I love you so much." He held her upwards and downwards while massaging her buttocks pulling them close together. "I love you too", she said moaning and crying out. Maliek stroked Jada until sweat begin to pour down his face. She kissed the salty taste of the sweat that rolled down his face. He moved faster feeling her juices begin to flow. "I'm coming baby." He felt the head of his manhood enlarge until it begin to mix with her juices. "Oh, Maliek this is so good."

"Um huh, Um huh". He came again. He kept her on top of him while they kissed passionately until his weakness begin to take over his body. As he lifted her off of him, "what am I going to do with you, Jada?"

"Just love me the way you do. That's all." They got out showered and had a nice dinner once they got upstairs in their extra-large bed, Maliek made love to Jada again.

Afterwards, they held each other for the rest of the night.

Chapter 37

Maliek called Ali early the next morning to see if he was going to bring Tracey with him. He told him yes. After hanging up, he told Jada to call the wedding planner Genesis to stop by. He did notice that his brother had taken an interest in her the night of the dinner. He also had Sung prepare some steaks and corn on the grill and told him to make sure he made a salad so that Jada could get the right nourishment. He turned on his stereo. It was installed all around the whole grounds of the mansion. So when they get on the court, they could hear the music. He knew James loved Jazz music. So he found Bob James' CD and this would be just perfect for the occasion. Everyone arrived right on schedule. His brother looked real different this time. He wore Nike shorts and matching top and gym shoes to match. He topped it off with a Nike hat. It's one thing the two brothers have in common. They always dress to perfection. Ali looked at both of them and said, "I know yall didn't think that I was going to be left out." They looked at him up and down in his Roca wear short set. "It doesn't matter. I can put on one of my Armani suits and gators and whip both of you all." Maliek said laughing, "I got some gators in my trunk. Do you want me to go and get them?" James said, "let's do this." They headed for the court. While they were playing ball, the three women sat outside and chatted about the wedding. "Girl you got it made", Genesis said to Jada. "You think so", she replied.

"Yeah, I think so too", Tracey said.

"Do you all want to go swimming? It's real nice and it will be fun."

"We didn't bring anything to swim in", Tracey mentioned.

"Girl, I got everything a person need to wear in swimwear in my little room by the pool, men and women, and guess what? You get to keep them." They went and got dressed out for the pool. All three came out looking like they could pose for Jet magazine. Once the guys finished, they came to join them at the pool. James couldn't keep his eyes off of Genesis especially in that swim suit she was wearing. Being with his brother meant the world to him after all of the years of separation. They got in the water and played like they used to racing back and forth. After everyone showered and got dressed again they had a nice dinner. "Man you all are welcome to stay all night if you want to", Maliek offered. Ali and Tracey agreed but James said, "man I would but I have to be in service tomorrow."

"I can't but one day, I will take you up on that offer", Genesis spoke. Both of them got ready to leave at the same time. Maliek hugged his brother. "Man, I really enjoyed you today and I want to do this all the time. James was still as cool as ever. He gave his brother some dap. "You got that, bet", James walked Genesis to her SUV truck. "I had so much fun today and I must tell you again to come to my service again."

"You know I think I will take you up on that offer", she told him after he shut her door. He walked to his car. She watched him, shaking her head, "um, um um". They drove off at the same time. Ali and Tracey decided to go to the theater to watch a movie. He asked Maliek and Jada if they were going to join them. "No man, we have some rated X movies in the room we are going to watch." Ali said, "yeah I know", pointing to Jada's stomach. At least Ali and Tracey started out watching the movie but if anyone was standing outside, they would have known it wasn't just the movie that sounded rated X.

Maliek and Jada got in their bed. He turned on the plasma television that was mounted on the wall. He turned to the XXX rated station that his satellite picked up. "Maliek what are you watching", she said. She knew the look in his brown eyes. She has seen it plenty of times. It was on for sure. He striped her of the Victoria Secret's gown she was wearing and crawled on top of her kissing each inch of her body. She watched the movie and it made her just that more heated. She wanted to perform like the model on the movie. "Lay down", she told him. He laid down and she eased in between his legs and grabbed him with her right hand and started rubbing him up and down. She massaged him while putting her lips on his tip. She moved her hand and began to go up and down on him. Maliek's eyes widened. This was the second time Jada had performed this on him. When he took her to Paris was the first. Playing the movies was teaching her how to be a professional. She sucked him up and down until his veins began to pop out. She watched him looking into his eyes while she performed. "Ohhh baby", he moaned. She went at a faster pace. "Jada, Jada". She got aroused from the sound of him calling her name. Maliek couldn't take it anymore. He raised up and go behind her entering her. She could feel the throbbing of him as he went in. "Ohhh", she cried. "Maliek!" He stroked in and out of her. She joined the rhythm pushing back on him. They moaned and called out to each other. Both of them hollered. Jada's face laid in the sheets. Maliek collapsed on top of her until he felt his last drop of fluid come out. He pulled out and laid her down. "Baby, did I hurt you?"

"No, Maliek. I will let you know if you do. I want it like that and it was just like when we was on that train in Paris."

"Yes it was, sweetheart. Wait here. I will go get a towel. Don't move."

"I couldn't if I want to. They cleaned up and fell asleep with laying in his arms.

Chapter 38

Monday morning rolled around fast. Maliek and Jada had the weekend of their lives. They got dressed and headed for the court house. When they reached the stairs Ali and Tracey were waiting for them. "Man I see you didn't forget", Maliek told him. "I wouldn't miss this for the world." Tracey and Jada hugged. "Girl are you ok", Tracey asked her. "Yes girl, ready than ever. I just want this to be over." They took the elevator to the third floor. The judge was sentencing someone else. They seated themselves. Once they called Doug's case number, they brought him out. He was very red in the face. He had grown a beard. Looks like he hadn't shaven in quite some time. They called Jada to the stand and made her put her hand on the bible. "Can you identify the man that was involved in the kidnapping?" She pointed to Doug. As she was returning to her seat, Doug looked around and said, "what's up, sweet cakes". Before anyone could blink Ali and Maliek were on him. "Order in this court!" "Boom", banged the gavel. "Order! Order!" The guards restrained both men and they were ordered out of the court room. Doug with a busted lip looked at Tracey and said, "I will be out to party with you again", then we winked his eye at her. Ali started at him again and Maliek grabbed him. "Let him go. He will get what is coming to him where he is going and probably will wear eye shadow". Don't drop the soap", Maliek said with a sly grin. They left the courthouse glad that this part was over. One down and one to go. Doug was found guilty and sentenced to ten years for his part in the kidnapping. He looked and saw his neighbor sitting in the courtroom. He asked his attorney if he could have a few words with him. He assured him that he would look out for him and put the rest of the money up. Doug could really do his time knowing that his money was in safe keeping. "You know that's why I have always trusted you, man." They escorted him out. "I will come to see you Mr. Doug". Court was adjourned.

Chapter 39

CJ sat contemplating on his next move. He dialed Des' number. "Hello", he said.

"Hey CJ"

"Well, I want you and Juquan to pick me up so I can take the both of you out to eat."

"CJ, I'm a little tired. I don't know if that is such a good idea"

"You know what, Des? I am getting tired of you always having some kind of excuse to be with me lately. What has gotten into you?"

"CJ there is nothing wrong with me. Check yourself."

"Are you coming or what?"

"Ok, just this one time. I don't feel like getting into it with you." She really didn't want to go but she knew he would only get pissed off and probably come over clowning. She had not yet quite figured out how to deal with him. She got Juquan ready and they left to pick him up. They drove in front of the house and blew the horn. "Ma, where are we", Juquan asked with his head tilted to the side showing nothing in his eyes but curiosity. When he saw CJ come out the house, "what is my Daddy doing over here?"

"I don't know baby." He acted like he understood. His eyes lit up at the sight of his dad. Most kids don't care what their parents do, they have unconditional love in their hearts for them. Once CJ got in the car, he asked his son where he would like to eat. Juquan picked Applebee's. Every time he sees the Applebee's commercial, he would tell Des, "I want that, Ma". They had a nice meal. CJ watched Des all during the meal as if he wanted to start in on her but he know what was best for him if he even thought about acting out in front of their son. After they finished and got back in the car, "why don't you drop J off at Nana's house? I really need to talk to you." She did what he asked to keep down the confusion. While they rode in silence back to his place, he asked her, "Des so you don't want to be bothered with me anymore, huh?"

"No, it's not that CJ. I am just being a little careful. And you have started back drinking and you know how I feel about that."

"That is not an excuse, Des. What about my needs? He didn't have to spell it out. She knew what he wanted. She also knew that she had to stay close around him to know his every move. "Stop at the gas station so that I can get a newspaper." She stopped at the nearest store. He glanced through the paper and his expression changed, seeing a picture of Doug made his heart do a flip. The article let him know that Jada was supposed to testify against him earlier. "Now that was today", he said. "What was today", she asked. "Your brother's girlfriend was supposed to testify against the man that helped me kidnap her today." He continued to browse through the paper. The next article he read made his eyes get even larger. He saw that Maliek was to wed

Jada next weekend. It took him into deep thought. She parked the car and glanced at what he was daydreaming about. Once they made eye contact, he had a smirk on his face that she didn't like. Des went in with CJ and didn't stay long. She gave him a little bit of what he wanted just enough to stay close to him. She watched the ceiling the entire time. It wasn't that she didn't love CJ but when he gets in this state of mind with all of the drinking, she did not want to be around him. Once upon a time, they used to have great sex together and were the perfect couple. When she told him she was leaving, he seemed to cop an attitude but she didn't care at this point. She tried to think of a solution all the way home. Once she was in her driveway, she noticed that the card her brother gave her wasn't on the dashboard where she placed it. "Oh no I know he didn't take that card", she said to herself. She went inside and called him on his cell phone. "CJ did you get a card off of my dashboard?"

"Why", he answered in a smart tone.

"What are you doing with his card anyway? What are you trying to set me up or something? Now all of a sudden you are riding around with your brother's card. Where did you get it from?"

"It doesn't matter where I got the card from. The point is, CJ it don't belong to you."

"Well, it does now", he said hanging up on her. She shed some tears before going next door to get her son.

Chapter 40

Over the next week, Maliek took Jada to the club with him everyday and they enjoyed every minute of each other. They made love all over the mansion. She missed her Mom and Brother but Maliek filled in quite well. They were real excited because this was the week of the wedding and in a couple of days people will start flying in from everywhere. Maliek had large friends all over the world and none of them would miss this event of the century.

Chapter 41
The Week of the Wedding

Everyone started flying in the Thursday before the wedding. Chi Chi had planned to come back earlier but she delayed her flight until Thursday morning. Jada decided to pick her up from the airport. She walked through the airport, glamorous as ever. Jada spotted her. "Hey girl", Jada hollered through the crowd of people. Chi Chi could recognize that voice anywhere. "Jada, I didn't know you were going to pick me up. I was looking for your driver."

"I am so excited about my wedding. At least I can pick my best friend up. Let's hurry. My car is right in front and I don't want them to give me a ticket." They jumped in her white Lexis and drove back to the mansion. Once inside after Chi Chi got settled in, they went over the last wedding plans and everything seemed to be in order. Chi Chi phoned all of the girls that they chose to be in the wedding. Jada had no idea that Chi Chi had big plans for her. Mom and Aaron arrived after lunch. When Aaron saw Chi Chi he asked her, "where is your hubby?"

"He couldn't make it", she told him. Jada looked at Aaron and changed the subject. "How was everything at home?" Mrs. James said, "he wasn't around very much, he was chauffeuring that car around. He has never had a Benz. I guess the one he owns is old, but it was in very mint condition. You all should have seen him. He looked like he was a movie star and all the women in Benton Harbor thought he was. They started ringing my phone all times of the night. I guess they thought he was back in the NFL league. I kept telling them to call his cell phone and stop disturbing me. "

"Oh Mama, it wasn't quite like that. You know I have always been a very popular guy standing at 6ft 3inches tall with a true athletic build." What stood out most was those muscles were still in tack. He thought he would lose that after his accident but he seemed to manage it very well. "Jada", he said, "I have a question for you". Is it ok if I bring Regina to the wedding?"

"Who are you talking about? That thing from the club", Chi Chi said exposing her jealously. Jada looked at them both as if to say stop it you two and said, "sure I don't see why not Aaron." Mrs. James kept watching the plasma television that was mounted on the far wall as if she didn't hear a thing. Aaron's cell phone rang and he tried to talk low. He had a choice to walk out but for some reason he didn't. "Yeah, I'm back and I miss you too. Yeah, tonight we can do that", he closed his phone with a smile. He looked at all three of them, "well duty calls". Chi Chi rolled her eyes and Jada shook her head. He kissed his Mom on the cheek. "See you later, Darling." She loved the attention her son gave her. He loved his mother. He waved at Jada and Chi Chi. "Bye", he said walking out of the door smiling. He thought "if looks could kill."

"I have an idea", Jada suggested. "Why don't I take you and Mama to Motor City Casino on Grand River Ave. "So we can have a little fun and Mom would you like to invite Sung to come along? Just say this will be in appreciation for just being so good to me for all of you." They all got ready to go out for the rest of the evening. Sung was so excited that he didn't know what to do with himself. He never got out too much. He looked very nice wearing his Armani Exchange white button up shirt and blue jeans. Also he sported a pair of Ferragmo loafers everyone took a second look at him. "You can tell he work for my man", Jada said once they were in the Lexus. Sung smelled so good that no one could smell what they were wearing. "What is the name of that cologne you are wearing", Mrs. James asked him.

"Oh, just a little Burberry cologne". Jada was watching them in her rear view mirror. She and her mother's eyes locked together. "My kids are a trip", she said. Jada phoned Maliek on the way, "yes I have enough money", she told him. That didn't sound good enough to him. He told her, he and some of his friends would meet them there. She didn't mention Sung was with them. She wanted it to be a surprise to him. Maliek was forever trying to get Sung to go places but he was so dedicated to making sure everything was in order at the mansion plus preparing all of the meals. The casino was really off the hook. Maliek arrived with about fifteen people that came from out of town. He even showed up with Pierre and his lady. The last time Maliek and Jada were on his island, Pierre told them he wouldn't miss this wedding for the world. Everyone had a lot of fun playing slots and gambling. Maliek was so generous that when anyone's money got low, he offered to give them some to splurge. They all saw the love he and Jada shared. A match from heaven. Maliek had a lot of friends who came from the Dominican Republic and Columbia. He rented an entire floor at the Hilton for many of the guests and the rest stayed at the mansion. Once everyone was full of drinks and won some money, they all headed to their destinations for tomorrow will be the big day before the wedding.

Chapter 42

Everyone woke up early. Chi Chi , Mom, and Jada left at eight o'clock to get their hair done and manicures. Deb really put the whip on their hair. When they got back to the mansion, it looked like a whole construction crew was there. There were delivery people and set up crews for the garden. Genesis was running around with her check list. That girl really knew her stuff. Maliek had already left to meet up with his friends that flew in for the wedding so they could pick up their suits he had delivered. Chi Chi and Genesis came up with a getaway plan to throw Jada off. It worked. When they reached the condo, Aaron left the door open like he was asked. The decorating team was in and out within two hours. They headed back to the mansion before Jada got suspicious and started to ask too many questions. She had phone them once already. Chi Chi told Genesis, "girl Jada is too much. Can she just let me give her a surprise?" They parked and got out of Genesis' Navigator truck. Chi Chi phoned all of the girls at the hotel and told them there will be limos there to pick them up at five thirty and that everyone should meet in the lobby. That was all set.

After Maliek returned home, Jada watched her man get dressed for his bachelor party. He selected an Armani two piece shirt style top and pants with matching Mauri shoes. She asked him, "how long is your party going to last?" He looked at her as he brushed the waves in his hair. "Baby, I don't know what the guys have planned for me." She was looking as if he was going out with another woman. "Come here you", he said outstretching his arms toward her. After hugging her, he looked down at her directly in her eyes, "baby you got the man there is nothing for you to worry about."

"Ok but", he cut her off by placing his lips on hers and stopped whatever she was about to say. "I'll see you later, sweetheart."

"How much later", she asked.

"Tomorrow at the wedding."

"Oh, so you are not staying here tonight?"

"Yes, I am, but I will be sleeping in the white velvet room tonight. You know I can't see the bride before the wedding."

"Ok, I guess you are right. I will miss you", she told him.

"I will miss you too." He gave her one more kiss before leaving out of the door looking like he was going to the Grammy Awards. Jada got herself dressed and she couldn't have looked any lovelier. When she got downstairs, Chi Chi and Genesis were looking like the cat that swallowed the Canary. "What", she said to both them. Mrs. James came in and gave her a gift bag. "This is for you".

"Mama, you didn't have to".

"Yes, I did. You are my only daughter". She wouldn't be going with them but she knew what Chi Chi had planned. She told her earlier. She loved the idea, but she had not planned to tire herself out before the wedding.

Chapter 43
$$$ Maliek's Bachelor Party $$$

Maliek arrived at the club around seven thirty. All of his friends were waiting downstairs. Ali and Aaron walked outside to meet him after Goldie radioed them. "What's up", he said to them. "It's your night", Ali spoke when they walked inside the club. Everyone started going to the third floor. Once the elevator came back down, it was time for Maliek and Ali to get on the elevator. When the doors swung open, there were two young fine stallions dressed in cowboy outfits with cowboy hats. "Let's go man, he told Maliek smiling at the look on his face. "I'm Cinnamon", one of the girls said. "And I'm Spice", the other one said. They grabbed each side of his arms. Once they reached the third floor, there were eight more dancers dressed in the same outfits. The guys had the place decorated in black and white, silver and gold. There was a king chair with steps sitting in the middle of the floor covered in all gold with silver specks sparkling out of the covering. They had temporary poles everywhere. There were so many guys that Maliek hadn't seen in a very long time and some that he didn't know. This place was full to its capacity once everyone was seated, they started the show of the century. The girls started off slow to the music of T Pain's, *I'm in love with a stripper,* while the fellas got their drink on. There was nothing served but Moet, Pipers and Cristal. Maliek was really enjoying himself. He really brightened up when he saw Sung walk in. Sung nodded his head toward Maliek while checking out the women climb the poles and drop down. His friends and everyone else acted like they were getting married the next day. Ali got on the microphone, "may I have your attention gentlemen". Everyone got quiet. The doors flew open and two of the dancers had changed into all white costumes with shingles swaying as they rolled a large cake right in the middle of the floor. The two started dancing on each side of the cake. Now Spice jumped out of the cake moving every inch of her body to the sound of one of Maliek's favorite songs by R. Kelly, *Bump and Grind*. He stood up on the steps that were placed below the chair. He was enjoying this last night so much that he started dancing in the chair. The guys were hollering, "go Maliek, Go Maliek". He had all of the dancers surrounding him for a couple of records. He told Ali, "man you really got me this time. I owe you big time."

"No man you don't owe me nothing. Just be happy." Maliek was looking around to find Aaron. He had one of the dancers cornered off all night getting himself a private show. The party lasted until two o'clock. Maliek, Aaron, and Ali were walking out at the same time. Maliek told him, "I thought one of the dancers was missing half of the night". The all laughed.

Chapter 44

While Maliek's party was going on, all of the girls met up at the mansion. "Listen up ladies", Chi Chi said. "Now that everyone is here, load up in the limo and you all can follow me and Jada." Jada was in shock not knowing what was going on. "Where are we going", she asked.

"Don't worry about it, Sweetie. Just enjoy the ride." Chi Chi walked out to the garage and pulled out Jada's Benz with the convertible top and picked her up in the front. They all caravanned to Jada's condo. "Girl, why are we at my condo?"

"Jada you ask too many questions". Chi Chi popped the automatic lock. "Come on girl. Trust me." Once they got inside, Jada didn't believe her eyes. They had the place decorated in wedding colors, purple and white balloons and banners everywhere. They had two fine muscular built waiters dressed in black and white serving hors d'oeuvres and champagne. The girls were giving her gifts and they were experts at choosing the right gifts for this occasion. Jada sat with teary eyes. No one knew what Chi Chi and Genesis was up to the next. The music changed in volume and Maxwell came on, *A Women's Work.* The waiters put their trays on the built in bar and started stripping and rolling their fine, fine bodies. All of the women started to scream and especially Jada. She could not believe what she was seeing. "Girl, you are the best friend I ever had", she told Chi Chi, hugging her. "And you know it", Chi Chi replied. After half of the young ladies were horny enough to go back to the hotel to wear their men out, they left. The guys introduced themselves as two of the Chippendales; Sexual Chocolate and D_Sex. No one would have ever figured them out with the waiter uniforms on. The party ended at one forty-five. Jada and Chi Chi were all worn out from all of the excitement. This was one of the best shows a lot of them had seen in their time. "Jada you can take the limo back. I am going to clean up for awhile. I will drive your car back to the mansion."

"Alright", Jada answered before giving it any more thought. Chi Chi turned on the radio and grabbed the pack of garbage bags under the kitchen sink. 92.3fm is the station to soothe your mind this time of the morning. She was feeling good. She had her share of champagne. She walked to the patio and opened the sliding glass doors. There was fresh breeze of early morning air blowing. She stood there enjoying the view for a minute. "Let me get back to work." She turned to go back inside and someone was coming in with a key. She hesitated at first then she realized that it was Aaron. "What are you doing here, Chi Chi?"

"Oh, just cleaning up the mess from Jada's surprise bachelorette party. Aaron you should have saw the look on your sister's face when the waiters that was serving the party turned into the Chippendales and started stripping".

"What you all had the Chippendales?"

"Yes, Genesis knows them personally."

"No, you should have seen Maliek's expression when he realized he had some of the top dancers in Detroit. His party was off the hook."

"Oh I bet that was nice", she said. "Well Aaron, I have to finish this work so I can get back to the mansion."

"You want me to give you a hand", he asked her.

"Sure, in that way I can get finished quicker." They began to pick things up. He stopped, "Chi Chi about the last time you were here. I am sorry. I shouldn't or we shouldn't have been carrying on like two teenagers. Plus you are a married woman."

"Don't worry about that Aaron. It's like water under the bridge." Once they had cleared the dining room, they walked into the kitchen to put things away. "Well, we might as well have a night cap." He poured them one last glass of champagne. "Here's a toast to our friendship", the two glasses clanged together. They drank slowly. He put his glass in the dishwasher and turned to walk away. "Aaron", she called him grabbing his arm. She kissed him before he could ask her what she wanted. She put her glass on the counter while they continued to kiss. The kiss only made her want him again. He led her to the dining room and she took off her Victoria Secret thong and started to unbuckle his pants. He was more than hard. He was harder than a rock. He sat her on the dining room table and raised her legs. As she began to lay back as if she was in a bed, he pulled her all the way to the edge and began massaging his part around in a circular motion against her clit. "Is this what you want", he whispered. "Yes, I need it". He then entered her and started going in and out of her. He grabbed her by her shoulders. She started panting louder, calling his name. They were so busy that you could hear nothing but moaning.

Raymond felt bad after telling Chi Chi, he wasn't going to be able to make it to the wedding. He grabbed her condo keys that she left hanging in the kitchen and hopped on the next flight to Detroit. He thought he would make it up to her by surprising her. Once he got to the airport, he rented a landrover to drive. "I should never let her down knowing that this was an important day for her", he thought to himself. He had no problem finding the condo. She talked about how to get there so many times. When he drove up and verified that this was the correct address. There were two Benzes out front. He was glad that she left her keys hanging in the kitchen. If she wasn't at the condo then someone would know where to find her. He walked up to the door. Sounded like someone was having a good time. The music was playing at a comfortable tone. Once inside, the dining room was not visible from the front. The noise he heard made him think he should have rang the doorbell. He walked in the dining room and there was his wife laid out on the table with her legs up in the air and a man banging her for dear life. They didn't see him at first. Raymond couldn't stand it anymore. "Chianti what are you doing?" Aaron pulled out of her and she rolled over on the floor. "Oh Raymond, I'm so sorry", is all she could manage to say. He just stared at her. "I knew I shouldn't have married you. You are nothing but trash and I fell for it. I know all you wanted was fame and a man with money. I should have listened to my parents. I married you too soon. And man, I am not even mad at you nor am I going to fight you over this tramp. Matter of fact, you can go back to what you were doing. I am otta here." He threw the keys at Chi Chi and walked back out of the condo. He got back in the rented truck and drove back to the airport and boarded the next flight to Hartsfield airport in Atlanta. Chi Chi looked at Aaron who was in a bit of shock. "Aaron this is not your fault this time". She ran out the door and drove to the airport to see if she could catch up with him but when she arrived the flight had just taken off. She did feel bad but what could she do. The damage had already been done. This is something they would have to try to work out. While she was driving to the mansion, her mind kept replaying the look he had in his eyes. It was unforgettable. She kept thinking, "why did I mess around on my husband?" She still couldn't figure it out but for sure it was part of his fault for not spending any quality time with her at home. It's away, practice, practice, practice. She parked and went inside directly upstairs and this time she didn't cry herself to sleep. She was in a state of mild shock. Also when it wears off, she still would have to face reality and she made up in her mind that it will be after her best friend's wedding. Even this would not spoil the happiest day of Jada's life.

Chapter 45

!!!!!!!!!!! The Wedding of the Century !!!!!!!!!!

Jada rode down the long driveway in an all white carriage led by a white horse with a shaded purple tie with a bell around his neck. The young driver was dressed in all white with white gloves. He stopped the carriage in front of the garden, got down and opened the door for her. Aaron was standing there dressed in white with shaded purple. He took his sister's hand while smiling at how beautiful she looked. Her dress was an original by Vera Wang, all white with pearls going around the neck and V shaped back pearls covered her five foot train. Genesis walked up and connected her train as they began to take their long walk. Aaron said to her, "Jada you look like Cinderella".

"Why thank you, Aaron. You look rather handsome yourself." Jada had a real crown on with diamonds and a short veil just enough to cover her eyelids. They continued to walk as three hundred guests stood watching them. Mrs. James sat in the front row and she was shedding tears as they walked past her. Aaron winked at her and smiled at the end of the aisle. Under the beautifully decorated arch stood Maliek and his brother along with Ali and eight groomsmen all of whom were dressed in white tuxedos with white silk shirts and shaded purple ties and cummerbunds with white gator shoes. Chi Chi was wearing a shaded purple original gown by Vera Wang with the same V cut back as Jada's gown, lined with pearls and purple shoes. All of the bridesmaids wore shaded purples mixed with white gowns with purple shoes. They all wore the gift Jada had given them which was white pearl earrings and the necklace and bracelet to match. Maliek stood and watched his bride until he exchanged hands with Aaron. He couldn't stop looking at his Goddess he was blessed with. The Reverend began the ceremony. The two of them repeated their own personal vows while the guests listened and shed some tears at the beautiful couple uniting as one. James passed his brother the rings which were all gold and platinum. She was already wearing the ten carat diamond to match the set. The couple said the I Do's within a bling of an eye. "I now pronounce you man and wife. You may kiss the bride." The kiss the bride kiss was so long that the audience started applauding louder. "Ladies and gentlemen. I present to you Mr. and Mrs. Maliek Montana". Maliek had a surprise that none of the wedding party knew about. He led them to the back of the mansion and there were six hot balloons waiting with drivers. Genesis unfastened the train from Jada's dress. "Genesis did you know about this?"

"No, Jada. I cross my heart." Maliek told Genesis to make the announcement that they would return shortly. She smiled at Jada letting her know that she did know and it was her idea. "Maliek what are you up to now?"

"Don't be scared baby. It's only a little ride. Just like when we are on the plane."

"No Maliek, this is different but as long as you are holding me, I will be ok."

They all were securely placed and the balloons took off in the air. The guests watched in shock. Everyone began waving. The whole wedding party left gliding across Detroit. Once everyone seemed to relax, they started enjoying the ride. You could see people below stopping their cars waving at the beautiful sight. Jada stood in front of Maliek while he held her tight. Some of her veil blew lightly in his face. Once the balloons reached over Bell Isle which was the destination. The balloons touched down slowly one after the other. People stood in amazement watching. Limos were waiting to transport them back to the mansion. Jada's wedding present was sitting in the water. An all white baby Yacht with the letters Jada #1. She started crying while grabbing him around his neck. "Maliek, you didn't."

"Yes, I did. I just married the woman of my dreams. What did you expect? You know I believe in doing it big." The wedding party took a quick tour of the baby yacht. It was well put with all white leather furnishings with a bar and two cabins, one master with a private bath. "I know you all don't want to leave but we have to get back to the reception."

"No man, I don't want to leave. This is what I want when I get to be a grown man, Maliek. I want to be just like you", James said. Everyone loaded up in the awaiting limos and headed for the mansion. When they got back the mansion, the grounds were jumping, even the kids were having a good time.

Chapter 46

CJ put on his suit and toupee that could pass for a mini afro. He took the colored contacts out of his eyes and got rid of the mustache. He stood in the mirror and took a look at himself. He was very impressed, "yeah that's it. You look like a million dollars", he thought in his sub conscious mind. His cell phone rang. It was the limo driver he found in the yellow pages. Really it was the only one in the whole city that would take cash. "I'll be right down", he said grabbing his Bossalini hat. He stuffed his smith and Wesson inside of his jacket pocket and walked to the limo. While riding to the mansion, he was thinking how he really had outdone himself by going in a limo. It made him look a little more inconspicuous.

Desarie sat in her living room looking out the window thinking about how perfect it would be for her to show up at Maliek's wedding and let her brothers know she was their sister. She rehearsed the line several times of what she would say over and over. She dialed CJ's number. He didn't pick up the first time. He called her back and told her he was kind of busy. She tried dialing him again. No answer. All of a sudden a strange feeling came all over her. She knew he was not up to anything good. Plus, she was leary about this being her brother's wedding day. She was glad he left the newspaper in the car otherwise, she would have never known. She dialed him once more. Now she couldn't trust this. She went in her bedroom and got super sharp and hurried out of the door. She drove to where CJ hideout was. She got out of the car and rang the doorbell several times with no answer so she began knocking. The man next door came out of his house and asked her, "are you looking for the new guy upstairs?"

"Yes I am".

"He just left in a stretch limo, sharp as a tack."

"Oh no", she exclaimed. "Thank you sir", she said running to her car. She jumped in her Caddy and pulled off. All the way, she prayed, "Lord please don't let CJ do something stupid. Let me make it in time. I should have known he was up to no good when I saw the look on his face after he read the newspaper." When she arrived at the gate, a well dressed gentleman asked her, "Ma'am do you have an invitation?"

"No I don't need one. This is my brother's house." He was one of the hired guys for security for the wedding so he did not bother to argue with her. He let her through. She parked and grabbed her purse containing the letters from her mother to their father that would prove to her brothers that she was indeed their sister. She saw so many people partying and drinking champagne and talking. She kept walking looking through the crowd trying to see if there was anyone that resembled her husband. Maliek and James were standing in front of the camera taking pictures and laughing. She walked toward them. That's when she looked to her left side and recognized that style and his bowlegs. She knew them well. He pulled out his gun and aimed it towards her brothers. Des lunged in front of them. "Nooo CJ" she screamed. The bullet tore right through her stomach. Before he could do anymore damage, Ali was on him. "Don't move", he said pointing the gun to CJ's temple. He took the gun from him. James flipped his phone and dialed 911. Maliek walked over to CJ, "man you just don't get enough do you? Take him to the empty guest house."

"No I am not going anywhere until I see my wife. I shot her. She was protecting you all. That is you and James' sister I shot. She can't die. She can't die. She is the mother of my son." Maliek thought he was talking out of his head. The ambulance arrived followed by the police. Before they could get CJ anywhere, Maliek hit him knocking him to the ground, "and that is for messing with my family". Ali stood with his gun pointed wanting to shoot him so bad until his hands were shaking. James started talking to Ali, "man give me the gun. He is going to get what is coming to him. He is not worth shooting. Give me the gun." He looked at Maliek then passed him the gun. Maliek explained to the police that this was the FBI Most Wanted Man for kidnapping his wife. The police cuffed CJ and put him in the car. All you could hear was "Des, Des please don't die. I am sorry. I should have left this alone."

Chapter 47

Des was put on the stretcher and losing a lot of blood. Jada stood by the stretcher to see who this strange woman was. She told Jada in a weak tone, "take my purse and read the letters. You look beautiful sister-in-law." Jada didn't know what to make of this. James and Maliek walked over to where she was and she began to tell them the strange things this lady was saying. "This is the same lady that has been coming by the church." The ambulance drove off. Jada pulled out the letters. Both of their eyes widened to the sight of their old address with their father's name on the front. Maliek grabbed his brother's arm and led him inside the mansion. Jada followed behind them. Once inside of Maliek's study, they began to read the letters. "Oh my God", James said, "like we really have a sister. Let's go!" Maliek said "Jada stay here and make sure the guests are ok. I will call you as soon as I know something." He kissed her and the two brothers left to go to the hospital. When they reached the hospital, they went to the emergency room. "Do you have a Desarie Turner", they asked the middle aged woman that sat looking over her glasses. "Yes. She was just brought in. There is a team of doctors working on her. Are you immediate family?"

"Yes, we are her brothers", James said. She got on the phone. "Yes we have to rush her into emergency surgery." After three hours of surgery, one of the doctors came out to meet Maliek and James. "We were able to retrieve the bullet but she is very weak".

"Can we do anything", Maliek asked. "Yes, if one of you or both of you matches her blood type, you can donate blood". The two of them were led to the room where tests were given to see if their blood was a match. Once they finished, they went to the floor where their sister was transferred. The nurse told them one at a time but they weren't trying to hear that. They both entered the room. She was very sedated but she could see them both. "You are here". Each one grabbed one of her hands. "You both look so handsome. What a lovely wedding."

"Don't try to talk", Maliek said. "We are not going anywhere".

Chapter 48

As soon as Chi Chi got back to the mansion, she went upstairs. She would leave Jada a note letting Jada know she had to leave immediately. Now it was time to see what the outcome of her marriage would be. No one saw her but Aaron. He followed her to the room where she slept. He knocked lightly. She opened the door, "come on in Aaron". She continued to zip up her LV luggage. "Chi Chi I want you to know I am very sorry about what happened. If you want me to talk to your husband I will, man to man. She kept getting her things together while listening to him. She went in the bathroom. He was still talking. She hollered through the door, "this is not your fault. I have to deal with this. Remember, I kissed you first." She walked back into the room and stood in front of him. "I can handle this", she said.

"Don't you think you should let him calm down a little before you go back home?"

"No, I don't. I know what I am doing, Aaron".

"Well at least let me take you to the airport."

"Ok, Aaron, you can drive me. I am leaving Jada a note. Let's keep what happened between us. Is that a promise", she asked him.

"Promise. My lips are sealed", he replied. He picked up her luggage and drove her to the airport. As she was getting out of the car, she told him, "remember what I said."

"I got you, girl. Now go get your husband." She boarded the next flight to Hartsfield airport. The whole flight gave her enough reflective time to think about what she was going to say to him. Once she landed, her car was still in the parking lot. She drove to Alpharetta. When she got to her street, she started driving real slow noticing a Hummer parked beside her husband's Excursion. "I wonder who can that be?" She grabbed her luggage and went inside. She sat her bags down in the foyer and started up the stairs. She could hear voices, "stop Raymond". "Huh, a woman's voice", she opened her bedroom door to her hubby. He had the young model; the same one that he introduced her to at their wedding banquet. They were having deep sex. He had her in the back so she couldn't see Chi Chi. Right away, Ray noticed his wife from the mirror on the bed. At first he acted like he wasn't going to stop. "Oh so you are going to do this in my bed, Ray?" At the sound of Chi Chi's voice, the young model pushed him off of her and grabbed her clothes off the night stand and ran out of the door. Ray stood there and started putting on his boxers and house slippers. "You have the nerve to screw in our bed. I guess this is revenge, huh, Ray?"

"Look at you, Chi Chi just finished getting banged by god knows who and you come all up in here like you are surprised? Well let me tell you some more news. This is not the first time I have been with Tasha. Have you ever really thought about me being gone all of the time for practice? Now you know what I have been practicing." Chi Chi got so heated that she grabbed the lamp off the stand and threw it at him hitting him on the head. He picked up his pants and t-shirt off the floor and noticed his head was bleeding. He left out of the door walking down the steps. "Chi Chi, I am not going to fight you. I will hurt you. You can have it. I am done!"

"Finished!" She stood at the top of the stairs hollering, "I'm finished too. We never had a real marriage anyway!"

Chapter 49

Maliek and James sat at their sister's bedside wearing the same blood stained Tuxedos from the wedding for hours but neither one of them cared. They have never felt so close to her now. James told Maliek to grab her hand. He grabbed the other one and began to pray, "Lord I know that everything is in your hands and I ask that you spare my sister's life just as you did ours. I am asking that you give us a chance to know her, Amen". The two brothers were very saddened with teary eyes. "She is so beautiful", Maliek said. "Yeah, she looks a lot like Dad", he replied. "Let's go home and change and we will come right back", Maliek suggested.

"Ok". They took another look at her and kissed her on the cheeks then walked to the nurse's station and gave them their numbers and walked out the door.

CJ made the ten o'clock news. Agent Jones and Knoles stated that they were on his trail all the time but we know that they take credit every time. Over the next few weeks it was touch and go for Desarie but her two brothers never left her side. Nana kept Juquan and tried hard to answer his questions. She kept telling him, Mommy will be home soon. The three of them became real close during the following weeks and finally coming to terms that they had a long lost sister.

Chi Chi and Raymond split. She kept the house. Jada was trying to convince her to move back to Detroit.

Epilogue

Five months later at a family dinner at the mansion. Desarie and Jada were sitting on the terrace while Maliek and James played touch football with their new nephew that they adored so much and Juquan loved them. In the years to come both men would play a big part in his life. He called them both "Uncl". They really loved that. Jada screamed "ooohhhh", then there a gushing of water that splattered hitting the floor. "Get my husband, Des the baby is coming!" She ran to the field to get him. When he heard what happened his heart dropped to his knees. They ran to the mansion. Maliek told James, "let's get her to the hospital".

"I don't think, I have time", she said. He phoned the midwife. At first he wanted the baby to be born at home but over the months he and Jada changed their minds. The doctor instructed them to take her to a room on the first floor of the mansion. Maliek was so nervous. James and Des were doing all of the work. Dr. Schram arrived as her pains got to one minute apart. James and Des stood outside the door. They could hear her scream in pain. Mrs. James and Aaron were just pulling up from a weekend trip home. They started not to go because it was so close to Jada having the baby but they made it back just in time. When Des told them what was going on, Mrs. James rushed to the room to help Maliek coach her. "Push, Jada", her mother told her. "I am trying. It hurts so bad, Ma!" Her mother felt bad but there was nothing she could do. This is all a part of child bearing. The doctor told her, "Now take one hard push with all you got." She did and out popped a little boy! Maliek was sweating more than Jada. The doctor passed the baby to Mrs. James. Maliek walked out to tell them the news. While he was gone, Jada felt another excruciating pain. The doctor said, "looks like there is another one!" She pushed again and out popped a girl! Maliek walked back in the room and saw another baby. He passed out in the recliner for a few minutes. Once everything was over, that was the happiest day of all of their lives.

Juquan told Desarie, "Ma, I got two cousins to play with now, Maliek and Malieka".

"Yes, you do, sweetheart".

Made in the USA
San Bernardino, CA
18 June 2016